I AM MACHINE

LESSON ONE
LIFE WITHOUT FREE WILL

LEX VAN DER PLOEG
RAYMOND VAN AALST

SCIENCE AND FICTION FOR EARTHLY AND EXTRATERRESTRIAL INTELLECT

Lex Van der Ploeg
Raymond van Aalst

ISBN: 978-1-955026-62-8

Published by Ballast Books
www.ballastbooks.com

We love to partner with new authors and bring their books to life.
For more information, please email info@ballastbooks.com.

To all who question existence:
For those in need,
act with speed,
clarifying capabilities
and free will inabilities,
to understand what we do
or fail to pursue
because we are built
and skilled
as conditioned intellect,
which we need to inspect
to help understand
where we land
when accepting life without free will,
which is a remarkable skill.
Your aliens will be here to help.
Don't hesitate—just YELP.
Galactic exploration:
It's life's new orientation.
Because we are not alone…
It's carved in stone.

TABLE OF CONTENTS

PART II
Ramona's Galactic Fantasy

PART III
Enabling Mathematical Principles

PROLOGUE

Eons ago, on a distant planet in our galaxy near the great globular cluster Messier 13, there lived an alien named Ramona Black Hole. Ramona's physique appeared equivalent to earthly humans, though her habitat and the space-time zone in which she lived were incomparable.

A critical factor allowing the development of superior intellect included that Ramona's lifespan tracked thousands of earthly years. Ramona's millennial learning experiences and intellect contributed to superior cognitive maturation when compared to human lifeforms.

Ramona's basic senses, from touch to smell, mimicked human capabilities. However, in preparation for her visit to Earth, Ramona required extensive adjustments to align her physical appearance with human lifeforms. For example, while Ramona had regular arms and legs, she had two pairs of six-foot-long fingered tentacles on her torso, which improved exploration of her environment. Prior to travel to Earth, surgical tentacle removal resulted in her overall bodily appearance being identical to humans. However, Ramona's skin was naturally oily and covered with scales, like a fish. Again, pharmaceutical treatment and surgery allowed her to change into an admirable human female beauty, meaning neither earthly men nor women would suspect her extraplanetary origin.

This philosophical alien contemplated that her life, while at times pleasant, remained full of unexpected surprises. Her entire existence, Ramona had wondered how her mind created feelings, emotions, and decisions. She compared her ability to act on observations, sometimes in a calculated manner, as intrinsic and comparable to what we know as human intelligence. However, Ramona realized that it was easy to conflate the intellectual freedom in decision-making with free will.

Ramona reflected on the free will definitions on Messier 13 as well as on Earth, which included the "ability to have done otherwise" or "an absence of constraints preventing one from doing what one wishes to do."[1] These definitions assume that the act of decision-making by a living organism equates to free will. In Ramona's opinion, this definition, when dealing with a conditioned mindset, will fall short of true free will enablement and is better referred to as "pseudo–free will." For Ramona, the phrase "pseudo-free will" involves accepting that genuine free will does not exist. While making a decision is seen as a free-will-enabled activity, Ramona theorized that all decision-making drivers are controlled and restricted by—or, better phrased, held hostage by—the body's design. Ramona found the concept of the free will fallacy exciting and endeavored to explore its intricacies.

1 (Hossenfelder and Palmer; Hume)

Joining the Galactic Exploration Team

Given great scientific advances on her planet, Ramona decided to join the galactic exploration team. This team, in a series of covert operations, planned to visit various planets, learn about other lifeforms, and explore free will in the universe.

Traveling through the galaxy and visiting other planets, Ramona soon realized that most living creatures, even those on Earth, where she had recently sojourned, represented conditioned machines enabled by machine-like artificial general intelligence (AGI).[2] To clarify this, Ramona concluded that the ability to observe and react enables living creatures to feel as though they are in charge and executing with free will.

However, Ramona ended up considering a contrarian viewpoint. For most of the organisms she encountered, their need to focus on daily living had prevented them from accepting the fact that *they are so busy staying alive, they fail to recognize that they have little to do with it.* Ramona observed that routine tasks, from cooking and eating to cleaning, washing, going to school, or performing a job to sustain living, make up 99 percent of the activities of the human population on Earth. *They perform these tasks because that's how they were built, and this is how Earth, their living environment, dominates activities. It's a closed circle with no way out where free will is a meaningless phrase.*

As a result, even Ramona ended up concluding that she also was an "observer" of the programmed actions taken by her body, her "machine," which came with a diverse but

2 (Goertzel' and see Ref: "Other 1")

prepackaged set of capabilities. These prepackaged capabilities facilitated the machine's performance within its environment. These considerations gave her personal identity and the pride associated with being a particular "machine" a specific meaning. This, in turn, helped her rationalize her own identity. While Ramona had many more years of experience and was enabled by the ability to change her physique, even she was dominated by her non-negotiable design. In line with this reasoning, Ramona could explain why she also experienced limited freedom in decision-making.

She learned from visits to Earth and other planets that many planetary beings refuse to accept the viewpoint that they operate without free will—that is, they act as the observers of the decisions taken by their conditioned "machine." Ramona concluded that, like fish trapped in a bowl, we are caught in our planetary living environment, enabled by annual trips around a sun. On these trips, planetary observations and Ramona's physique, her machine, determined her intellect and actions. Even at that time, little did she know, due to the constraints of her planetary fishbowl, or the earthly fishbowl, where she was headed.

Exploring Theoretical Lifeforms

Understanding the scope and limitations of intellectual abilities and behaviors allowed Ramona to consider what more advanced lifeforms might entail. Thus, Ramona began exploring theoretical lifeforms and searched for advanced intellect in our galaxy.

Ramona had assumed that imagination has no limits since it allows one to consider the implausible. However, even when fantasy roams wild, it is easy to remain caught in a trap built by experiences and preconceived ideas. Hence, imagination can remain confined by the nature of the physical being. In this endeavor, Ramona rediscovered the limitations of her own mind. She learned that intellectual capabilities and what appears "implausible" are dependent variables. As a result, stepping out of our defined cognitive world is hard to accomplish.

These issues are dominated by the body's, the machine's, physical design. The manner by which living organisms have developed, including behaviors from desire for propagation to hunger, are all encoded by the machine, which defines a being's ability to observe, create innovative ideas, or adopt novel intellectual concepts. Ramona learned that from love to careers or politics, the operating principles of the machine and its conditioning through life define each of us.

Societal Conditioning

Unfortunately, due to flawed assumptions regarding free will, most societies she visited had neglected to properly organize the training of their AGI machines. Generally, lifeforms go about their daily lives unwittingly conditioning their AGI machine. Most societies fail to recognize that their routine methods of communication and learning entail simple methods of conditioning the machine.

Ramona noticed that, on Earth and even her own planet, information received from governments or other groups, whether accurate or not, can develop a mindset that, over time, becomes almost impossible to correct. Once this has become part of daily life, this conditioning takes its own path and can be used to start social unrest and even wars. In seeking an example, one might look to the religion or political party one is trained to accept, leading to assimilation with its associated behaviors.

Given the status of most living creatures as AGI machines with a defined set of capabilities, the management of the machines leads to great opportunities and risks. For instance, Ramona visited many societies where AGI training and learning had done profound harm. To her dismay, she found rampant examples of inappropriate societal conditioning, including numerous activities on planet Earth. In this context, the dangers of inappropriate societal conditioning campaigns became all too clear to Ramona.

To be more specific, she was astounded by the wealth of examples that speckled Earth's history, most recently leading to the Second World War. Here, over a short fifteen-year period, devastating changes in core values were accepted by a small subset of Earth's population, referred to as the Nazis. However short the time period, the results were catastrophic with deaths estimated between forty million and fifty million and still more lives irreparably destroyed.

This reminded Ramona of the current politically oriented communication challenges on Earth. Where news releases and other information were meant to educate and unite beings, the methods applied were, in fact, dividing them. Recent political events on Earth had become ever more polarized due to non-factual rhetoric by political leaders, enabled by their news media. The dangers of such campaigns cannot be underestimated.

As a result, Ramona thought it prudent to propose to add a new clinical indication to Earth's Diagnostic and Statistical Manual of Mental Disorders, a condition referred to as media-induced mental illness (MIMI). To combat MIMI, Earth could create a new role for a planetary regulatory agency, including the Food and Drug Administration (FDA). The agency would reject or approve selected political speeches, control biased news releases, and prescribe mandated anti-psychotics and anti-depressants for key political figures or news anchors. That could prove enormously valuable in enabling and stabilizing societies as mental illness could be erased from leadership, instilling a core set of values to enable humanity's stable growth.

Too Much Ain't Enough – A Cognitive Power Principle

Selected events did shine a brighter light on Ramona's path forward. In the eighties, during one of her visits to Earth, she spent occasional time at a bar named The Lone Ranger in New York City. There, Ramona produced new insights. Rowdy crowds gathered at the popular establishment. Rattling motor bikes were the preferred form of transportation of The Lone Ranger's customers. The sign over the bar, which read "Too Much Ain't Enough," became a constant reminder of Ramona's mental aspirations and goals. The phrase captured her objective to go beyond conditioned knowledge in the search for advanced lifeforms and intellect. Unfortunately,

The Lone Ranger, "Too Much Ain't Enough." An earthly evening enabling fantasy in our universe. "Too Much Ain't Enough" is the core goal when building cognitive powers. Ramona had embraced the notion that, in attaining intellectual capabilities, "Too Much Ain't Enough" presents a fabulous vision. While the customers at The Lone Ranger translated "Too Much Ain't Enough" most often into immediate satisfaction through social contacts and alcohol consumption, Ramona had instilled wisdom in her attendance while visiting The Lone Ranger.

The Lone Ranger, while inspiring, did not accomplish its intellectual goals for most visitors at its boisterous, alcohol-fueled evenings.

On one of these evenings, The Lone Ranger hosted a special gambling themed event. Being mischaracterized as a gambler, Ramona was sucked into a conversation with a gambling fanatic who ranted and raved about the pleasures of tossing the dice. The conversation was quickly terminated when Ramona swirled her Pinot Noir and tersely stated, "I hate to gamble but love to win." Indeed, while Ramona's ability to place calculated bets had helped her make progress in life, the outcome of those bets was not left to chance. Ramona chose to stack the intellectual deck in her favor.

Flipping a coin through her fingers, she smiled to herself. *Intellectually, too much ain't enough can help improve the odds. There's always more to know. To learn. To observe. Under those conditions, that's a gamble I can take indefinitely on Earth or any other planet.*

Ramona's Efforts to Unwind Conditioned Biases Gain Traction

On her road of discoveries, Ramona's unraveling of earthly religious biases resulted in her publication of *God's Retirement: Lesson Zero.*[3] This illustrated comic for both believers and infidels, earthly and extraterrestrial intellectuals, opened the door to the realization that only the physical underpinnings of life stand as parameters to exploring the why, what, and how of life. As summarized elegantly by Richard Feynman, "There

3 (Van der Ploeg and Van Aalst)

is nothing that living things do that cannot be understood from the point of view that they are made of atoms acting according to the laws of physics."[4]

Sticking to the notion that life is made of matter where its physical properties explain all of life's capabilities leads to a few conclusions. Firstly, matter's ability to create complex, propagating, and evolving lifeforms leaves no alternative than to accept Ramona's dependency on matter's design principles. She argued that all that we see is a representation of parts of different lifeforms. For instance, planet Earth, its rocks, and its biological life are all representations of parts of different lifeforms. Each of these lifeforms interact with their environment over drastically different time frames.

And so, Ramona documented her journeys. Her trials. Her tribulations. Her observations. Ramona now has the privilege of documenting them here for you. In the next ten chapters, our alien resident will cover definitions, findings, and theories of life. Ramona will then compare herself, human lifeforms, and other lifeforms she encountered in our galaxy and our universe.

These are the building blocks for Ramona's memoir about life and free will.

---

4 (Feynman, Leighton, Sands)

PART 1
LIFEFORMS IN OUR UNIVERSE

Scientific Support for Life without Free Will

Chapter 1
THE HUMAN MACHINE

After arriving on Earth, Ramona realized that humans are charmed by what they observe but remain mentally confined. After all, staying alive is a full-time job. To Ramona, who had lived hundreds of earthly lifetimes, humans seemed asleep at the wheel, just living in a reactive fashion with the inability to wake up in order to see what life is really about.

Over a glass of something tasty to drink, Ramona jotted in her journal. *The very act of living prevents humans from recognizing that the clutter and complexity of 'being' is what keeps them occupied. They are like blind fish living in their earthly fishbowl.*

She paused, took a sip, and continued. *In this fishbowl, the concepts of free will and individuality are illusions. Humans' failure to understand that they lack input into matter's forces, which create their evolving design, leads them to incorrect interpretations of the concept of individuality. They also fail to see that all actions are dictated by the conditioned machines that these lifeforms represent.*

Ramona sighed and stared out her little window. *These beings have no, or only limited, input into a range of emotional capabilities. Staying alive and being functional in their environment defines all their actions.*

She went on to make the comparison that their minds, which operate similar to an AGI machine, are like a blind pilot in charge of a spaceship (or what they'd call their body). In this analogy, being blind restricts awareness of actions taken and their consequences. AGI machines, like the earthly organisms known as a whale, octopus, seagull, or human lifeform, all follow similar, standard AGI operating principles. Ramona argued that there is indeed no data to support the notion that any particular human lifeform is superior to any other lifeform. *They are all following a "design" where each planetary lifeform exhibits distinct capabilities. In essence, it is the ability to observe, influence, and shape the environment that represents the common feature of humans and most other lifeforms.*

In addition, Ramona stressed that these earthly lifeforms manage survival through the application of intellect and an inherent set of capabilities often referred to as instinct. Intellect, the human's evolved AGI, facilitates operational control under diverse and, at times, challenging conditions. Instinct is a non-negotiable, hard-coded capability of the machine.

Finally, she stated that the ability to apply intellect to calculate a course of action should not be equated with free will. Like Ramona, humans are the fortunate observers of the machine's actions with remarkably little operational freedom. *But what a pretty little fishbowl they live in,* she concluded.

Ramona comes from her planet in the great globular cluster Messier 13. On this planet, biological life replicates and multiplies like on Earth. However, selected advanced lifeforms on her planet developed the ability to construct or "print" a mature lifeform in real time from the physical elements. These printed lifeforms have an advantage as each follows the then prominent preferred design. Each new design, in its turn, is better enabled for required physical, cognitive, and behavioral capabilities and functionalities.

The improved design principles were derived from an array of lifeforms the galactic exploration team had encountered across the galaxy, taking what they interpreted as the best of all worlds and homogenizing and then replicating it for use. Given Messier 13's living conditions, many designs mimicked aspects of Earth's biological life.

Ramona was printed and started her life as a fully educated and well-conditioned adult, completely prepared for her planetary life. Ramona's blueprint designated her to be a philosophical researcher with superior intellect and social abilities.

Prior to travel to Earth, Ramona became an active member of the Messier 13 galactic exploration team, which she joined at the age of just over 4,000 years. Based on her printed physical design and the ability to implement some earthly adaptations, Ramona was well prepared for this role. As a galactic explorer, she was inquisitive, eager to learn, observant, and compassionate.

After arrival on Earth in the early 1900s, Ramona explained some of her viewpoints about lifeforms she encountered.

So, let me tell you what I experienced on my travels through different space-time zones. I'm currently analyzing life on Earth. One of my close earthly associates shared the following regarding what he felt about me while we were engaged in typical human sexual behavior:

"I felt her beauty. A deep emotional awareness came over me. I wanted to be close to her. I became fixated on her beautiful dark and long hair. Her eyes were mesmerizing. We drowned in each other's gaze and lost all sense of time."

Many sexual partners shared similar examples of these aspects of attraction, beauty, and desire during my time on Earth. I soon realized that these preferences were not created or developed by the individuals engaged in the observations. Each of them observed and learned from their preset menu of preferences.

Of course, this menu, over time, becomes enriched with experiences and data input. Humans act on these observations and pursue a path based on preferences, which are neither the observer's creation nor choice. The ability to act on a preference is presumed to reflect free will. However, the hard-coded preferences are, in fact, managed based on the "machine's" inherent design. Humans are simply willing observers of the actions taken by their preset menu of options.

An inroad to skepticism around the general interpretation of free will, for instance, also comes from the concerns raised by parents who have young pregnant teenagers or incarcerated youth. Here, due to the teenager's apparent impulsive behavior, one more easily questions the affected youth's free will concept. This becomes all the more obvious if one considers how drivers of any of these behaviors, like uncontrolled anger, sexual preferences, or intellectual abilities, are the reflection of the body's program enabled by local conditioning. This, for instance, includes the environment of childhood education or simple media-enabled data sharing. Interestingly, these issues are rampant in our universe, and lifeforms on most planets I visited suffered the same fate. Surprisingly, a few planetary lifeforms that exist in our galaxy exhibit superior functionality enabled by true free will, upon which I will elaborate later.

Like these examples of acting on emotion based on observations, Ramona documented a wealth of events of similar complexity (listed below).

First, why do humans eat and enjoy a meal? Every system is built to reward food-seeking behaviors, and the machine is designed to crave the rewards.[5,6] Why do many creatures in our universe have sex? Again, the system rewards the behavior and seeks the partnership, and the rewards leave us pleasantly astounded. Why? Behavioral rewards drive action and control the machine. Without these rewards, we would be stranded and unable to survive. Put simply, we act based on the anticipated physical and emotional rewards designed and granted by our AGI machine. Examples range from attaining the benefits of social status to receiving a verbal compliment or extra sugar in our coffee.

With her head bent, a light shining dimly overhead, Ramona scribbled away in her journal:

Interestingly, I have learned that these same principles apply throughout our galaxy and the universe. These drivers guide us, from drinking water to learning, communication, and other social activities.

While discussing these principles on Earth, these turned out easier to accept for humanity when considering, for instance, the fate of humans with genetic differences that

5 (Sapolsky)
6 (Tomlinson)

control extreme presentations of their machine's functionality. I learned on Earth that free will has nothing to do with the behaviors, capabilities, or preferences of people with autism spectrum disorder, Prader-Willi syndrome, Down syndrome, or severe obesity or those suffering from addiction or other compulsory behaviors. Each is an example of the human machine's condition. In their genetic makeup, we can often notice the drivers of such atypical behaviors. Most humans, however, only see the clinically diagnosed members of humanity as built with an inborn error while considering themselves without error or "normal" and free will enabled. All else are "defective" and, because of the defect, lack free will.

Based on that viewpoint, only those with "errors" exhibit predefined and unusual behaviors, which humans view as indicative of a lack of free will. We see these as "unusual" because some of these behaviors deviate from the norm. Human observers who consider themselves "normal" equate that to being in charge of their machine and executing with free will. However, based on what I have experienced, we must consider that those humans that are presumed to be "normal" are also built to fit a norm with narrowly predefined capabilities. Hence, whatever one assumes to be "normal" or "defective," no one operates with free will; we simply fail to be self-critical or recognize our behavioral drivers in detail.

Next, I applied this liberally in testing sexual orientations, as this is one of the easy inroads to evaluate a proportion of the male and female machines. After a couple thousand encounters, I can now, with great accuracy, predict all male or female sexual behaviors and preferences. Here, the machine shows a hard-coded predefined regimen of these interesting creatures.

For instance, I found it interesting that my sexual cues, my hips, breasts, smiles, or garments, simply attracted hundreds of men and women over a matter of a few weeks. My gaining traction became a fully predictable activity.

Also consider severe childhood hunger and obesity as an example. Children impacted by genetic forms of severe obesity can weigh many hundreds of pounds by age fifteen. Their machine appears to have been preprogrammed with ever-present hunger, making a focus on food and hunger an integral feature of their being. Free will has no place among their likes and dislikes for food or many other activities. Their ever-present hunger is encoded in their machine, and their choice of food is merely an execution on that preprogrammed plan. Their lack of social interaction in the presence of food is devoid of free will, as is the interest in social events rather than food, under such conditions for others who lack the genetic difference.

Similarly, the high incidence of aggression in subjects that experienced early life moderate head trauma and their disproportionate rates of incarceration reflect the body's execution on a defined program.[7,8] *Other examples include the high rate of incarceration for people suffering from a learning and reading difference known as dyslexia, an inborn condition.*[9]

In reviewing our behavioral capabilities, I have not yet been able to find features that could speak against these lifeforms being sophisticated machines[10] *without free will. While we often acknowledge, for instance, the genetically diagnosed*

7 (Mosti and Coccaro)
8 (Williams, Chitsabesan and Fazel)
9 (Livingston, Siegel and Ribary)
10 (Sapolsky)

as exhibiting behaviors that deviate from the norm, we need to realize that the term "normal" is based on the lack of a comparator group.

To bring this one step closer, consider why humans eat, speak, drink, read, listen to music. When analyzing preferences and actions by reiteratively asking, "Why did I prefer this behavior?" the answer to the question ends up overriding the concept of free will.

After years of exploration, I have concluded that chaos theory integrated with AGI machine learning will come close to describing the human machine and its coded abilities, including the lack of free will.[11]

Stepping through these considerations, it seems plausible that humans are complex machines operating based on fixed, pleasantly complex programs where emotions, motivators, and actions appear as choices derived from a menu of options. However, the menu and its basic programs are defined, and the likes, dislikes, and capabilities are prescribed at the start. The program will adapt and evolve as experience grows, enabling conditioning in humans' environment, all based on data exposure and programming capabilities.

Despite these limitations, most living creatures Ramona encountered experienced pride about themselves, as can clearly be seen from the pleasantly self-conscious MRI brain scan of one of her human observers.

Ramona recognized on her journey that the deeper one dives into these events, the more apparent it becomes that most of us have little insight into the drivers of our own functioning. The notion is that "I am machine" addresses many

11 (Green and Lavesson)

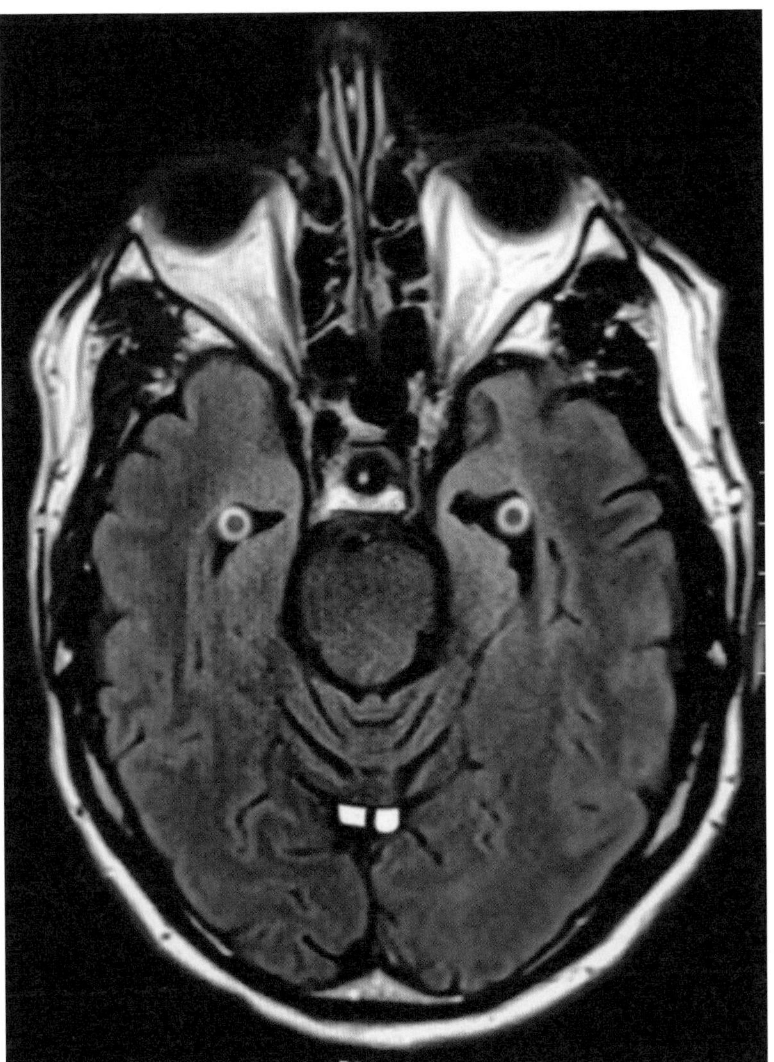

A human brain with a "rabbit" mind of its own. The human brain—an independent AGI machine. A close look by MRI scanning into the brain of a human colleague surprised Ramona as, indeed, this brain had a mind of its own, gazing at her with hungry eyes.

questions relating to behavior. The appreciation of what it is to be a programmed machine can improve the path living organisms take in their societies. For example, consider that the recognition that we are made to act by design and conditioning erodes the self-fulfilling desire of the megalomaniac or the guilt posed on creatures with criminal behaviors. They simply are caught by the faults of their design. This recognition allows for accurate planning and treatment before we face major issues, leading to stability across societies.

All of these lifeforms, whether they appear as whales, primates, or other living beings, follow the design of a chaos-theory-driven AGI machine learning system. Chaos theory combined with quantum mechanics invokes that none of these events are deterministic. We, in fact, do not know where we are heading. The bottom line is that most lifeforms we know are a complete design, a "defined package" that evolved in their environment as participants and observers. They had no say in their body or their planet's design principles. Behavioral routines are integral to the physical being, the machine. Partner preferences, feeding and social behaviors, as well as an array of key actions lifeforms take daily to sustain life are all defined by the premade machine.

While Ramona felt all this to be accurate, she wanted and needed to be more certain. She endeavored to find "hard evidence," something she could observe to make it true. She found just that evidence in cortical brain imaging, which supports the notion that the human brain activity needed in support of an action precedes the awareness of the action taken. The body, the machine, makes the choice prior to a lifeform's awareness of that very choice.[12]

Based on Ramona's experiences and interactions with diverse lifeforms, she concluded that lifeforms of all types tend to confuse the ability to act on a plan, impulse, or feeling or the ability to make decisions with free will. The perception of beauty, sounds, art, philosophy, and admiration of the environment are intrinsic features of the machine, not free will. These are reduced to practice in different forms for each of the population's representatives. These diverse abilities and observations result from the machine's complexity. Essentially, our machine dictates and drives our perceptions and value systems, where we are the observers of its decisions and actions.

The bottom line is that navigating life's challenges, coupled with preselected preferences and individual intellectual capabilities, allows exploration of an environment, a planet. This holds true, no matter whether you are an insect or a human primate living in our universe. We are all machines, preprogrammed, preconditioned, but able to accept a minutia of datapoints based on that very preprogramming.

Over her years on Earth, Ramona met many interesting people. One tenet held true: Humans have a human-centric view of what "life" entails. They assume that the time limits of observation and reactions they endure must be the norm for all lifeforms in the universe.

Ramona recognized that humans fail to consider the relevance or existence of other organic and inorganic lifeforms,

12 (Libet, Gleason and Wright)

Mr. PuTumP. An example of highly artificial general intelligence! Bottom line: Little did they know! Political AGI machines on Earth are often enabled with self-fulfilling prophecies of local grandeur, self-appreciation, enrichment, cruelty, and dishonesty. Mr. PuTumP represented an extreme example of these undesired capabilities, which a better organized society would treat at a local psychiatric clinic.

which can have lifespans covering thousands of years, whether on Earth or on other planets (see Chapter 2).

Ramona paused and tapped her pen on the desk. Why, there was a fantastic example of short-sightedness right in front of her. She had lived amongst the humans for generations, yet none assumed she was anything but human. She gazed out her small window and smiled while looking at a different though underappreciated lifeform: a stories tall, beautiful, strong oak tree. She pondered: *How many lives has that oak lived? How many humans have touched its bark? How many leaves has it shed? How many birds has it homed? How many eggs has it seen hatched?*

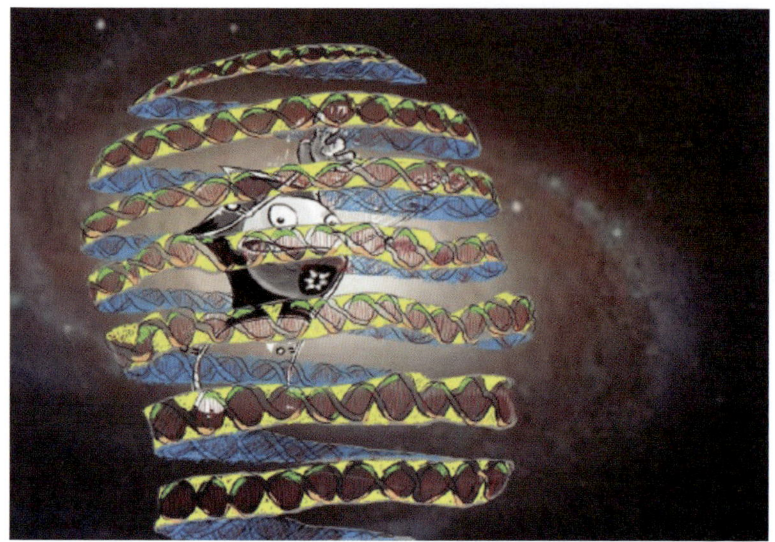

The universe with another example of a machine. This example is a biological design dictated by carbon dominated matter. Unlike human life, other lifeforms have life cycles that run thousands of years (see next sections). From organic to inorganic lifeforms, our universe is enabled by the atoms that build diverse living worlds.

Chapter 2

DEFINING LIFE

Based on what I have learned on my travels through the galaxy, I will now expand on how we can define "life." I will also make the case that lifeforms include both organic and inorganic versions. In addition, I have seen individual lifeforms unfold life's features over days to hundreds of thousands of years. Based on what I have learned, I define "life" broadly as the organization of physical matter into transiently self-sustaining higher order structures that induce chemical and physical changes in their environment.

Describing life's features in a broad sense helped expand my thinking. I consider organic life as self-sustaining and propagating matter, dependent on energy input for existence. In this process, lifeforms cooperate and can influence the physical makeup of their environment. Most organic life propagates through an information code that defines the lifeform's current state and evolution.

Inorganic lifeforms I have met comparably represent self-sustaining and propagating structures, dependent on energy input for existence, while, similar to organic lifeforms, influencing their environment. But inorganic lifeforms enable organic lifeform development and cooperation over long timescales. Inorganic lifeforms propagate through their core physical principles, not curtailed by a genetic information code.

Each of these lifeforms shares the ability to interact with their environment through intellect, defined as the ability to observe, integrate data, comprehend, learn, and react. These features are essential to the maintenance and propagation of organic and inorganic lifeforms, though the presentation of their intellect varies. Matter's ability to organize and spawn life represents one of the core capabilities of the physical elements in our universe.

Ramona stood at the front of a large lecture hall. Hundreds of eyes were staring intently at her. She took a deep breath and thought to herself, *I'm in a room filled with too much ain't enough. Let's give them a little more.*

"Hello, everyone! I'm Dr. Ramona. Let's focus on earthly lifeforms first…" And with that, she plunged into her much awaited lecture, "What Is Life?"

"All planetary lifeforms I have encountered require energy input to sustain life and to enable the process of propagation. Earth's organic lifeforms can influence their environment and are dependent on a 'nucleic acid code' to allow propagation and evolution. Just so you understand, on planet Earth, evolution of organisms is guided by the information in the nucleic acid code, their DNA, their genetics that evolved over billions of years.

"One of the core observations that stands out is the ability of organic lifeforms to exist as self-propagating systems relying on the carbon-atom-based nature of their chain of life events. These lifeforms can profoundly influence the chemical makeup of their environment through various functions that can include mating, feeding, social interactions, combat, and creating art. In addition, lifeforms often are essential partners in complex interactions. Such interactions include epidemics, ranging from Earth's malaria to SARS-Cov-2 infections. A key aspect of organic life is its intrinsic drive for propagation."

Ramona paused as some of the younger attendees chuckled and elbowed each other. How simple humans could be. How they could find joviality in the smallest, most impactful aspects of life. She smiled warmly and continued.

"Propagation is a basic feature of the system enabled by diverse parameters. For some lifeforms, propagation includes sexual activity and the need to be part of a community. 'It takes a community to raise a child,' is a human adage that speaks to the need to build a social structure for offspring maturation. These behavioral features are part of the coded 'machine' each of us, including myself, represents. While we are accepting of its features, we had no say in its design, whether as a human lifeform that developed on Earth or any other celestial body." Ramona paused and thought to herself, *like my own globular cluster Messier 13 design.*

"We all act based on how we were built to accomplish selected tasks. It is simply what we are. The question of why these coded life-enabling behaviors exist remains unanswered. Evolutionary theory only describes how the 'machine' evolved.

"A critical feature of life is what can be referred to as 'intellect.' Interestingly, this intellect is again a feature of the machine with all the preferences, likes, and dislikes inclusive of human's varying intellectual abilities."

Ramona tapped a key on her computer. The screen showed a stunning oil painting of human-like lifeforms in the universe.

Human-like lifeforms and their derivatives are thriving throughout our universe. Humans' DNA code exemplifies a generic tool enabling life-form replication. Humanity's likes and dislikes and the tools they developed all reflect their earthly confinement. Examples of earthly tools in our universe including cars, fetuses, DNA.

"These simple definitions can similarly be applied to inorganic lifeforms. An extreme viewpoint can be taken by defining aspects of inorganic lifeforms through their interactions with organic life, as is, for instance, becoming a reality through Earth's global warming."

As the grumbling mounted in the room, Ramona was reminded of the internal debate she'd had about using this example, knowing she would touch an exposed and raw societal nerve with the subject. However, watching the destruction of a planet she had called home for decades was enough to push her to use the example—damn the ramifications.

Over the din of the audience, Ramona raised her voice slightly to quell the chatter. "I will expand on this with the notion that each organic and inorganic lifeform is enabled by a display of diverse cognitive abilities. The argument that inorganic lifeforms express intellect holds true if we consider, for instance, Earth's response to human presence—say, for example, in observing and influencing the environment.

"Earth has provided a platform that evolves and allows a symbiotic fit for organic life in different biotopes, including oceans, lakes, and deserts. It creates, in this case, 'atomic comprehension.' Earth sustains a balanced microenvironment in support of diverse organic lifeforms. But what of Earth's role outside of itself?"

Ramona paused. The lecture hall had gone eerily silent. It seemed as if no one had considered that Earth served a purpose outside of itself.

"Earth's role in the universe may include transplanting lifeforms—through meteor impact, human missions, extraplanetary support, or other methods—to distant planets. Earth, thus, seeds organic and inorganic lifeforms and changes a recipient planet's balance. These planetary systems hold the foundational knowledge of what was built and generated over billions of years and what will come next in response to solar radiation or human presence. So, Earth reacts to the creatures present upon it, and Earth serves a purpose outside of itself.

"Interestingly, the same arguments can be made considering the impact of growing crystalline deposits that determine a matching environment for the next generation of deposits.

They influence their own environment by observing themselves and accepting or rejecting new deposits in various positions. These deposits have an intrinsic, or engrained, knowledge of what crystalline molecular building blocks will fit best. This is atomic comprehension, which comes with the fundamental knowledge of what has been, what can be learnt, and what will come next."

Ramona clicked a button on her computer once more. On the large screen in the hall, the attendees could see a jubilee of dancing crystals trying to determine where they could fit in together.

"They're cute, aren't they?" Ramona smiled at her audience and at the hundreds of machines before her. "Humans fail to see these inorganic systems as lifeforms. They fail to see the impact of these systems on their lives and environment—how they enable the propagation of organic lifeforms and how this has been performed over hundreds of thousands of years. Only now, with global warming, can humans choose to see the impact of changes in these inorganic 'objects' or, up to now, silent 'organs' of their earthly fishbowl. A human-centric viewpoint doesn't intuitively agree with the definition that planet Earth is a lifeform itself.

"Research I have conducted explains that even our galaxy, the Milky Way, can be considered an inorganic lifeform. Taking this a step further, even our universe with its diverse space-time zones, defined by gravity, fits the definition of an inorganic lifeform with the ability to observe, integrate, comprehend, learn, and react based on the presence of matter.

"We must consider that we, ourselves, are not much more than mobile complex atomic composites. We're acting on a

Smart crystals grab each other and build a mountain incorporating other crystal types. These crystal beds reflect sunlight and can moderate a planet's temperature. Meteors can move crystals between planets. This is atomic intellect! Inorganic lifeforms are underappreciated in many societies. Their impact will become ever clearer when, for instance, Earth, which is a vastly different, largely inorganic living creature, takes control of human life following global warming, rebalancing its habitat.

defined behavioral and evolutionary plan where we lacked input into our design and have little say in the choice, or the execution, of our actions."

Ramona preempted the crowd's disagreements. "After all, did any of you have any say into who your parents are? Any say in the genetics you inherited? The learning and conditioning you were exposed too?" Silence. Just as she had anticipated.

"Many organic lifeforms believe that they are dominant players in their daily activities, but there is little evidence to support this notion. By contrast, most of us are the observers of our predesigned machine's actions.

"Next, matter's ability to spawn replicates of a 'lifeform' represents one of the core capabilities of physical elements, whether organic or inorganic. Most lifeforms in our galaxy have an intrinsic program that maintains the state the lifeform has attained by replication to allow continuation of the process of their evolution. This holds true for organic and inorganic lifeforms, even though their 'life codes' are very different.

"Finally, a unique part of organic life on Earth may entail that such lifeforms exist to support the process of life's evolution on this planet and throughout the universe. This evolution of life relies on programmed cooperation and competition.

"Interestingly, the meaning of the word 'universe' captures these concepts, given its Latin origin meaning 'all together.' We impact all others, and all others impact us. We impact Earth, and she, in turn, impacts our ability to survive, to thrive. In a larger sense, consider that Earth is but one celestial body in a universe with an immense number of similar planets, each of which follow the same rules.

"Thank you."

Though hushed at first, the audience in the lecture hall stood up with roaring applause. Ramona smiled at the crowd. *Too much ain't enough. I hope I've spawned an era of curiosity and discovery*, Ramona thought to herself.

As she left the podium, she was hit with the realization that her discovery of parallel universes, which she had not yet disclosed to the audience, represented an entirely new era of thought that required elegant introductions so life on Earth could take this concept into account. Excitingly, this leads us to move from a universe to a multiverse and most likely a gigaverse!

Chapter 3

RECOGNIZING LIFEFORMS IN OUR UNIVERSE

Ramona sat at her desk, looking at an endless line of books and papers. They were strewn across her office, lining the walls, and stacked twenty high, making a maze to and from her desk. She sighed. *How could she help others understand that they must at least recognize the fact that Earth is not alone? It is not unique.*

Timelines and methods over which lifeforms reveal intellect and react to their environment can vary drastically. For instance, the definition of life and intellect defines planet Earth as a machine driven by geological and biological evolution. Humans, overall, fail to recognize Earth as a lifeform, as the timelines for Earth's responses to its environment, even humanity's presence, are significantly different from the shorter timelines of human life. For the latter, sharing of memories of social events spans several generations, after which the learning and social conditioning experiences tend to lose their impact on posterity. These timelines are not aligned with Earth's observations and reactions, which run hundreds to thousands of years.

In addition, the methods through which planetary lifeforms observe and even communicate information and the methods by which they react to their environments are vastly different and require exploration. As most earthly lifeforms have not yet considered their planet an intellectually enabled creature, Earth's methods of communication with, for instance, human life have been ignored. Soon, these methods will stand out and teach earthly lifeforms of the lack of balance through Earth's response to human presence.

Twirling a pencil between her fingers, she grasped for an example. *Earth's upcoming global warming calamities will demonstrate the planet's response to human life. Geological records show the unforgiving creature that Earth can present, providing humans with unexpected surprises, changing their habitats and social organization. It is likely that in Earth's existence, these changes will become a key example of a large population of living organisms being influenced by Earth's response, thereby rebalancing their presence. For instance, Earth's rapid loss of coral reefs and ongoing destruction of ocean life by vast amounts of plastic deposits will contribute to generating a new balance for life.*

Ramona paused to gather her thoughts before again scribbling feverishly. *Following this thought pattern, we could go as far as considering human life part of Earth's microbiome. These definitions erode a demarcation between classically defined life or non-lifeforms created by matter.*

She smiled, then frowned. *Now, how to make humans understand*? She continued scratching away furiously in her journal.

Inorganic matter contributes to the lifeform complexity that has developed on Earth. Inorganic life can be self-sustaining and propagating by building new chemical entities, such as the capture of carbon dioxide or the atomic comprehension of crystal beds in the Earth's crust. These activities are often dependent on energy input for existence and expansion. In turn, these inorganic lifeforms influence their environment through their core physical principles, which can lead to capture of sunlight or enable growth of organic life. These features describe the intellectual power of these inorganic systems. The drivers of, and the intrinsic code for, their propagation is simply defined in the inorganic nature of the atoms and the complexity of the structures created. Inorganic life is, thus, based on the ability of atoms to create complexity and share features of inorganic life with organic lifeforms.

Given the definition I have applied to organic life, planet Earth itself can be considered a living and intelligent organism whose actions and reactions span long time frames, ranging from hundreds to many thousands of years. This idea first materialized in the Gaia hypothesis.[13] *Planets like the Earth "observe and detect" and can "replicate" aspects of their design as well as "react," thus influencing their environment, representing an entirely different form of life with intellect.*

Humanity's role in this system is interesting but misunderstood. Humans view their role as central and dominant to life on Earth, its solar system, the galaxy, and the universe. This is founded on the importance given to "being alive," as defined by the self-awareness in the fulfillment of daily activities. This

13 (Lovelock)

interpretation is partially driven by the importance placed by humans to sustaining human biological life.

Now we need to help humanity understand their role as living organisms and compare this with the function provided by planet Earth as a living creature. We need to also reinforce that human life essentially equates to that of other organisms like whales, octopuses, dolphins, or eagles. All these organisms fulfill enormously complex tasks in their environments, where humans would fail at every step unless provided with suitable tools because they are not built to carry such roles.

A main issue that stands out is whether the organic lifeforms we represent are unique and serve a particular role in our galaxy or our universe. All I know right now is that we are part of the world of atoms that make organic and inorganic structures. This train of thought is similar to the earthly philosophies of panpsychism and panbiotism.[14] *To be clear, panpsychism proposes that every element of matter has a core of consciousness and is endowed with feeling, while panbiotism simply states that all matter contains life. This reasoning, of course, dictates that our universe is a lifeform or is teeming with lifeforms, be they organic or inorganic. My personal observations have fully corroborated this description, and I will follow up with some unique details in the next chapters.*

14 (Haeckel)

Earth is a lifeform and is part of trillions of other living planets in our universe. Expansion of our universe with even distribution of galaxies and matter has often been visualized as the distribution of matter in rising bread. As the dough expands, raisins in the bread move further apart in a uniform manner. So, we can model the movement of our galaxies as equally distributing throughout the universe, as if they are moving apart in the rising of the dough.

Chapter 4

WE ARE AMONG MANY

We live in a universe that is alive with organisms with an estimated six billion Earth-like planets just within our galaxy, the Milky Way. Our entire universe is enriched with organic and inorganic lifeforms.

Ramona knew this to be fact, but she struggled with how to help Earth's community understand that their life was not unique. Their lifeform was but one among trillions of others.

Frustrated and feeling destitute, she began scrawling in her journal.

In our galaxy, the Milky Way, hundreds of millions of Earth-like planets exist in the circumstellar or "Goldilocks" zone of sun-like stars. This is the area where one can predict that Earth-like, or Messier 13-like, life may develop. My understanding of lifeforms remains primitive, but I have been able to observe other organic lifeforms in our galaxy. In addition, I have been told by other extraterrestrials that such lifeforms flourish throughout the universe. Given this abundance of life, it is fortunate that humanity has largely escaped detection by extraterrestrials.

Following my visit to Earth, I now realize that living in stealth mode is good for Earth. Broader recognition of life-

forms by others in our galaxy or beyond would not fare well for life on Earth. Other civilizations with the advanced technical ability to reach Earth may not be interested in a nonconfrontational encounter similar to what my team initiated. My opinion is largely based on humanity's narrow viewpoint of its position in the universe and its poor global social organization.

The latter, of course, does not bode well for humanity's ability to generate a productive and well-coordinated response to even friendly alien encounters. Humanity still knows so little about what "life" entails that interacting with other lifeforms will have unanticipated consequences. These will likely involve social unrest, as nations will end up fighting for the prime position in representing Earth, and in case of a violent extraterrestrial takeover, Earth will face an inability to coordinate a timely global response. All in all, the restricted human viewpoint of earthly life prevents productive insights regarding the interaction with alternative lifeforms.

I became aware of Earth's existence due to an unusual Boltzmann brain event. The Boltzmann brain model[15,16] *predicts that the spontaneous, random existence of a human brain or any type of intellect anywhere in our universe with all cognitive capabilities, even for a fleeting time, is as likely as the existence of our universe. The model acknowledges that we could be the imaginary features of a Boltzmann brain. Through a short-lived Boltzmann brain event, I was able to share cognitive awareness in real time with an earthly man. I will refer to this phenomenon as "Boltzmann brain communication." What resulted was an astounding and profound experience.*

15 (Boltzmann, 1872)
16 (Linde, 2007)

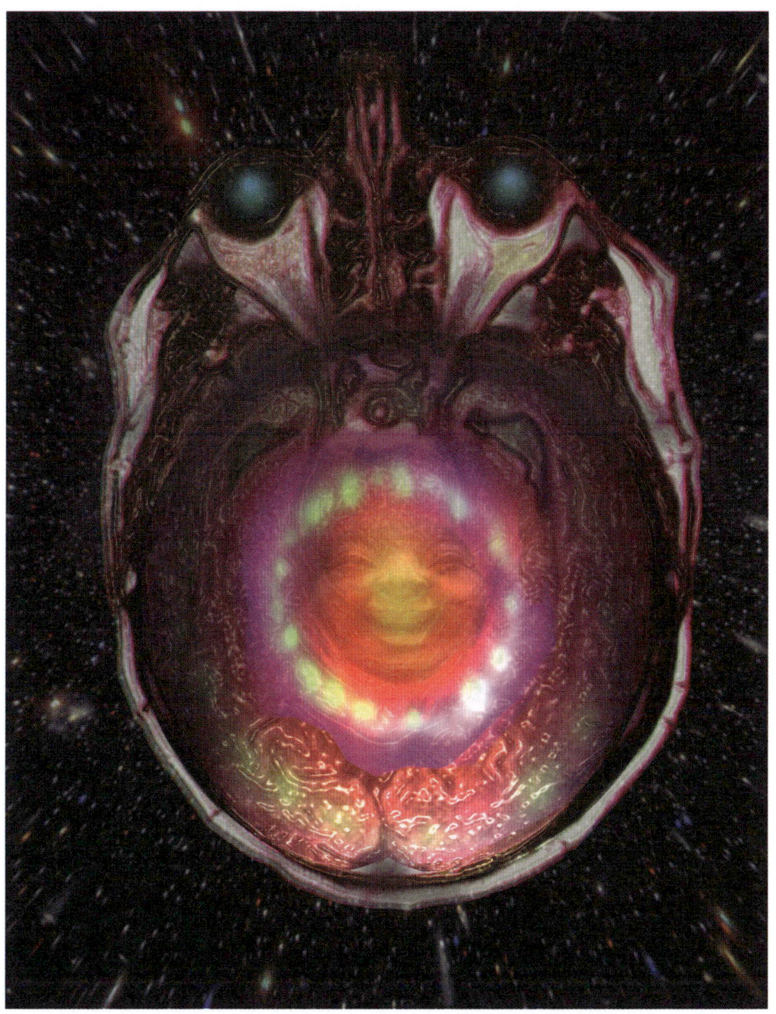

A Boltzmann brain in our universe. The spontaneous occurrence of intellect, a human brain, even for a brief period of time, has been proposed to be as likely as the existence of our universe. Consider the spontaneous occurrence of intellect that gathers the thoughts of organic life, like those of a married couple. Or consider the spontaneous collection of the thoughts and intellect of numerous living creatures. Ramona equates this with a superior form of intellect.

This created shared knowledge about life on Earth and its location. During this truly remarkable event, I was aware of two minds being merged in a time- and distance-independent manner, sharing critical information. As we were planning to visit Earth's solar system, my Boltzmann experience resulted in the galactic exploration team engaging in a careful analysis of the solar system's planets, leading to the discovery of planet Earth.

Many of us are carbon-based lifeforms. This process has repeated itself in many other settings, resulting in a diversity of lifeforms. Each has adapted to their own confined habitats in their own space-time zone where they evolved. These differences make communication and parallel evolution harder because these processes operate at different speeds in different stellar systems. While I have not encountered these, it is reasonable to assume that non-carbon-based organic lifeforms have also developed on other planets. Consider, for instance, the development of life based on another core element like silica-based life instead of carbon-based life or non-oxygen-based processes for energy input.[17] *Expanding our view of how atoms can create lifeforms will enable the discovery of next generation intellect. While these topics await further clarity, it should be obvious that we are just examples of a lifeform in our universe.*[18]

Notably, in our confined space-time zone, our perception of time is uneven, and individual experiences present excellent examples of this. The statement that time flies, sometimes verbalized by "I don't know what happened—it is as if years have passed in seconds," presents an interesting experience.

17 (Kuraoka)
18 (Leroy and Walker)

I have, at times, countered this with the statement that if time is going so fast, whether on Earth or on a different planet in our galaxy, it is probably not painful enough, as at least for me, time sure slows down under strenuous conditions. Hence, for the near term, earthly stress may be the best answer to the human experience of a time warp.

A universe teeming with life. Our galaxy is filled with diverse lifeforms of which living creatures on Earth are an example. Ramona introduces life on Earth to the presence of many lifeforms in our galaxy, representing organic and inorganic intellect.

Chapter 5

COMPLEXITY OF LIFEFORMS IN OUR UNIVERSE

Ramona gazed out over the top of Mountain Aoraki, previously Mount Cook, in New Zealand. Her eyes soaked in each and every tree, crevice, and speck of snow. The wind whipped around her and sent a shiver down her spine. Her companion, a human lifeform, hauled himself up to stand next to her at the peak.

As Ramona's eyes relayed what she saw and translated it into thought, she was struck with a realization. *Do humans understand how utterly un-alone they are? Are they able to understand not just that other lifeforms exist but that many of them are as complex, and as simple, as life here on Earth?*

Ramona turned to her human companion. "Looking out at this majestic beauty, I'm struck with a thought. Our machine's 'intellect' creates an opportunity for us to observe and interact with our habitat. I've hypothesized that several lifeforms in our universe are assembled and enabled with similar functional capabilities. If we consider the impact of evolution for life on Earth, I hope that humans can imagine that, in our universe, other lifeforms have developed, each in their own space-time zone. Such lifeforms will have varying levels of insight over what it means to be alive and, likely, some will have human-like 'observer' capabilities."

She paused as the cold wind licked at her face and snowflakes dotted her black hair. She took a deep breath of sweet, fresh, untainted Aoraki air.

"Taking this logic a step further, I assume you can imagine that many of these lifeforms represent different AGI machines. These machines each have a range of intellectual capabilities that evolved under their own unique evolutionary pressures. If that's the case, let's consider that if Earth is a lifeform that responds to its environmental exposures, though over exceptionally long time frames, other lifeforms exist in our universe, and they also have vastly different capabilities, including timelines over which they interact and evolve."

Ramona turned to her companion. She could see in his eyes the awe of the astounding beauty by which he was surrounded. She could also glimpse a speck of understanding at just how small he was in comparison to this one environment on Earth. Her lips turned up in a gentle smile with the knowledge that she had helped someone else appreciate their infinitesimal smallness.

Yes, Ramona thought, *this is what the next chapter must focus on. But, for now, I won't consider the spontaneous, non-evolutionary driven occurrence of Boltzmann intellect. Boltzmann intellect has a key difference; it is predicted to take on diverse intellectual capabilities that don't require evolutionary forces, at least as we understand them, to define its state.*

Ramona and her companion clambered back down Aoraki and pitched their tents in the dim evening light. Then, she crawled into her tent, pulled out her leatherbound journal, and began to write.

A favorable interpretation of human life is that it can consider itself an observer of life's processes but has no say regarding life's direction or design. By contrast, humans believe they are in charge. This assumption holds their societal and individual behavioral maturation hostage. In addition, their design and the landscape they operate within leave them fully reliant on their coded machine.

Like most lifeforms, humans are strolling blindly through their mental desert, only enabled by their personal predesigned, conditioned capabilities and preferences. It is not different for me. Most actions taken by our bodies, including cognitive, endocrine, metabolic, cardiovascular, or gastro-intestinal functions, are maintained without us even being aware of the intricacies needed to drive the continued functioning of the machine each of us represents.

Limitations are numerous as we are narrowly restricted by our evolutionary design, best captured by "what you see is what you have." For instance, our body's systems overall do not provide an effective early warning system for buildup of damage that precedes system failure. For each of us, our bodily functions move uninterrupted until we notice a system failure, which can manifest physical illness, ranging from cardiovascular to renal disease, or behavioral or social events, like depression or anxiety related disorders. There is no check engine light for our machine, nor do our machines exhibit advanced cognitive abilities enabling us to predict or calculate with any level of accuracy the actions of other creatures. There is no innate, built-in Magic 8 Ball. We assume that our bodies lack this capability because the evolutionary advantage of such a warning system was not part of natural selection.

A blind man in the desert. Humans, like many other lifeforms in our galaxy, are blind to their origin, destiny, and design limitations. Tracking a path through life is a daunting task in machine learning! Given humanity's intellectual and functional limitations, it has not been possible to elegantly track a course through life while considering what it means to be caught in an earthly fishbowl. Here, humanity completes its daily tasks in an uneducated and often distasteful manner.

Similar to earlier considerations, other limitations apply. For instance, we have limited capabilities to calculate the likelihood of certain future events, which can influence a system's survival or well-being. To manage environmental changes and allow us to function in our environment, our machine allows us a limited capability of external observations. Limitations, for instance, include that we only perceive some narrow spectrum of the radiation to which we are exposed.

For me, this is slightly different. While on Earth, I need to wear special optical lenses, as my natural ability to detect UV and other frequencies of Earth's light spectrum is much broader. Humans also only sense some odors, and again, I needed extensive surgical modifications to fit in with life on Earth. Furthermore, humans have limited tactile sensing and acoustic abilities and can taste only some nutrients. Unlike humans, I have the fortunate ability to precalculate some aspects of my system's functioning and can prevent certain system failures. I can also redirect system's decisions guided by my enhanced ability to accurately calculate the likelihood of certain future events. These capabilities present primitive aspects of free will enablement.

Most of us, including myself, have limited abilities to observe and read the behavioral intent of others, and we have variable communication skills. In addition, most of us have little to no control over our dietary and behavioral preferences, as exemplified by humans' preference for alcohol, sugar, drug use, partners, and/or other conditioned abilities. Each of these can be highly detrimental to our machine, yet we still seek them out. We still use them. We still want them. This logic implies that our observations and the machine's function in its environment are intimately linked. As humans react based on the awareness of their senses, these abilities have led to the assumption that these observational and cognitive capabilities define life.

To further explore these topics, let's consider what other lifeforms have evolved in our universe. I will describe a gradi-

ent of lifeforms, one of which is theoretical, even for me. I will start with the most advanced proposed lifeform, which I have not yet encountered.

Firstly, I have posed a question regarding whether there are forms of intellect that can have real-time input into their system's design, including on-demand oversight of their system's controls (the conditioned preset behaviors). Recall that we are all machines with a control system. That control system is conditioned with preset behaviors and remains relatively set throughout life.

But what if a lifeform could have real-time input on that system to adjust its design based on potential future needs? Such a lifeform would be capable of decision-making that is independent of its system's design and, hence, would be enabled by genuine free will.

I refer to this as a system's "design independency." Yes, the system was designed at the outset, but this lifeform can rewrite its system. This system's design independency requires an intricate ability to precalculate critical aspects of life's processes, estimate the likelihood of predicted future events, and adjust the system's capabilities to be optimally prepared for those future events. This process requires a dynamic system that can develop condition-dependent capabilities.

While I have traveled broadly in our galaxy, I have not yet met this type of lifeform. Based on the rules we know, such a lifeform, be it organic or inorganic, would need to have evolved from existing matter. Again, based on what we currently know, the development of such a system would represent a clear evolutionary advantage. However, from the perspective of known lifeforms on planets in our galaxy, this type of advanced system's design evolution is at first hard to conceive. Despite this difficulty, selected scenarios deserve consideration.

For instance, we could imagine enhanced functionality through real-time, flexible, need-driven, organismal cooperation. A simple nonconditional version of organismal cooperation can be found in the human's microbiome, which enables life through enhanced nutrient absorption, development of intellect, and gastrointestinal-hormone-release-driven emotions. In addition, social cooperation among groups of organisms can represent primitive types of adaptation to realize enhanced intellect and functionality. Examples include the coordination of activities living organisms engage in when hunting or farming or the nutrient-seeking behaviors of insects.

For more advanced lifeforms, we can consider the ability for distinct organisms to physically merge to exhibit enhanced cognitive and physical skills in real time. Such cooperative organisms would likely have an evolutionary advantage and, potentially, condition-dependent, superior intellectual capabilities. Alternatively, the spontaneous occurrence of Boltzmann-like superior intellect presents another example, though this needs to be seen outside of lifeform evolution. Here, the Boltzmann brain that engages the intellect of hundreds of living organisms may with great accuracy calculate its next activities based on an array of viewpoints and experiences.

Secondly, in this hierarchy, there are systems with constant full knowledge of the system's functional activities but without the ability to influence or redirect its functional design on demand. This system provides a superior ability to control its system's decisions. This, again, represents an aspect of genu-

ine free will. This level of control requires detailed system insights. As a result, it has intellectual independence over many of the system's design principles, which can otherwise dictate its actions.

While this was originally conjecture, I was able to meet such a second-level lifeform near our Galactic North Pole. Though I was unable to complete my diagnosis and analysis, its functioning was mind-blowing, providing me with valuable insights and allowing me to engage on my current mission of planetary lifeform observations.

Nimble Bee, as I came to call her, was a three-foot tall, wingless, insect-like creature. She wasn't what humans would call beautiful, per se, but she was remarkably stunning in her intellectual abilities. She was able to respond to observations in a manner that appeared almost independent from her physical design.

I named her "Nimble Bee" as she was unimaginably well-organized with a super fast intellect, tracking real-time observations and, in conversation, immediately sharing well-calculated plans at a high pace in my own language, even though we never actually spoke. What I mean by that is, we shared our cognitive powers, our minds and thoughts, in real time.

I imagined that Nimble Bee simply had the ability to calculate with great accuracy the best path into the future. She seemed able to define which events had a high probability of occurring, and these "predictions" helped shape her future.

Nimble Bee was, by earthly standards, over 4,000 years old. She attained this age because her ability to manage system functioning prevented system failures. In addition, Nimble

Bee's intellect and decision-making were not dictated by her physical design, and she was able to conceive and explain ideas not limited by her own physique. For Nimble Bee, "Too Much Ain't Enough" had become an intellectual reality!

Nimble Bee was immediately aware of my issues en route to Earth and advised me to undergo the necessary surgeries and physical adaptations so that I could function optimally and fit in with the population on Earth. Nimble Bee's feedback was so elegant and complete that I had no questions. All was addressed in a heartbeat, as she was able to measure my abilities and limitations expertly. I walked away with a world of admiration for her being.

The third level narrowly describes my own capabilities and entails limited knowledge of the system's functional drivers. However, I retain some ability to control and guide system decisions. At this level, the system still requires application of logic and superior analytical capabilities and is enabled by aspects of free will.

The fourth lifeform entails limited knowledge of the system's functional activities and is guided purely by observational and reactive capabilities without detailed knowhow of the system's functional drivers. Life's input here is in the ability to fine-tune system functioning in its habitat. This level entails much of the human-like behavior and intellect.

The fifth level addresses limited knowledge of the system's functional activities with restricted observational input to system decisions. This level represents lifeforms whose actions are largely dictated by evolution driven programs with limited system awareness. These functionalities resemble many of those seen in creatures on Earth as diverse as snails and crys-

tal beds. Here, the lifeform manages execution of predefined tasks. Other examples of these lifeforms include plants, bacteria, and other observationally and cognitively impaired organisms.

Please note that we must be careful with this interpretation as the cognitive power of these systems is easily misinterpreted. For instance, plant life on Earth can be seen as an essential organ of the lifeform that Earth itself represents, just like our bones are an intricate part of our bodies. If so, we may misjudge the role of essential "organs" like forests.

To recapitulate, these lifeforms, from bottom to top, entail: (5th) execution on cooperative complex chemical and biochemical functions with limited system awareness, (4th) observer abilities, (3rd) manipulation of life's direction capabilities, (2nd) control of life's direction, and (1st) full system design and control capabilities. I have encountered levels two through five in our galaxy, and I am optimistic that, in our universe, this diversity of lifeforms flourishes.

To give this a personal note, myself and most forms of human life represent level-three and level-four evolved lifeforms. With my current knowhow, it remains hard to accurately place Earth as a lifeform on this scale, as it could fit levels three through five.

Finally, considering life's design principles, I need to stress that, in this universe, the fundamental matter that we are made of may be adjusted or manipulated to derive yet a separate set of building blocks, as defined in the periodic table of elements, potentially leading to distinct forms of living matter (see Part II).

PART 2
RAMONA’S GALACTIC FANTASY

Chapter 6

THE CYCLICAL UNIVERSE

Ramona awaited the arrival of the galactic team members at her apartment on Earth. She had set out her favorite Earth treats and drinks. Upon their arrival, the galactic team shared their experiences regarding their earthly lifeform observations. The team members had experienced diverse encounters with the human machine in different geographies across the globe. Their shared experiences and careful measurements further solidified the level four lifeform measurement for humanity.

Soon after their Earth summary meeting, the team prepared to return to their planet near the great globular cluster Messier 13. Returning to their home planet was critical for their next exploration of the galaxy with the aim to explore life beyond the boundaries of the Milky Way.

To return to the globular cluster Messier 13, each team member scanned their current earthly physical and atomic composition and transferred this information to their planet near Messier 13. Using a portable scanner, their physical forms were digitally captured, and their atomic makeup information was relayed instantly to their planet using advanced time- and distance-independent quantum communication capabilities. Back on their planet, each would then be reassembled from the digital information provided. Following reassembly of their lifeforms near Messier 13, their earthly bodies were designed to disintegrate and evaporate in a matter of seconds.

As a result, later that morning, the galactic team was back on their home planet near Messier 13 and prepared for their next endeavor. Interestingly, Ramona noted that this form of transportation had, in some form, been considered by Konrad Zuse, a German civil engineer on Earth, though it had never been put into practice.[19]

While Ramona was ready for the team's next grand galactic adventure, she deeply valued the lessons learned on Earth and therefore maintained her apartment for the coming decades. During that time, she traveled back to Earth for regular meetings with her earthly group of friends.

Her reasons weren't entirely self-serving. In addition to visiting friends and The Lone Ranger, the plan was to introduce some members of her human network to the galactic transportation capabilities and to invite some on selected journeys through the Milky Way. However, this required sharing of the galactic team's true identity and disclosure of its mission details.

The team decided to postpone this foray until their next exploration of planet Earth aimed at enabling improved social conditioning of earthly societies. This task was planned to be initiated over the next fifty years. The timeline was a bit tricky, however. It required Ramona to assume that planet Earth could survive this period without self-inflicted destructive behaviors, the latter being an unfortunate behavioral feature of numerous societies, which the team had observed and become all too

19 (Zuse)

familiar with on their explorations of organic life in the galaxy. Nonetheless, Ramona had some level of hope in humanity.

While Ramona had advanced the complexity of lifeform considerations during her explorations, the ultimate answers to the why, what, and how of life remained largely unresolved. Frustrated, Ramona decided to pursue her next quantum travel trip to tackle these critical issues. She considered that the answers to her questions could be found if she could travel outside of existing space and time. This would allow her to look back and reflect on "existence" and "life." Ramona's fantasy about this path inspired her to consider that such a journey would unveil crisp answers.

While there are several theoretical roads one can walk to get these explanations, Ramona had no interest in tracking the generally accepted path through end of life or death. Many humans and other organic creatures anticipated resolution to such philosophical questions at that point in their short lives. However, in Ramona's mind, an answer was unlikely to be found at the time of death.

After all, she thought, *we are matter-based machines composed of atoms. While Boltzmann-enabled cognitive powers may provide key insights, the bottom line is that all we can expect to learn is based on the power of the atoms we are made of. Death of a living organic organism bypasses the power of atomic observations. It's a one-way journey into absolute nothingness.* Stated differently, death is not a path to clarity on any life-based observations; it is merely the end of everything. Fortunately, Ramona's conclusion was elegantly supported by recent thermodynamic considerations refuting the existence of hell or heaven for most living creatures. In an exquisitely funny essay, an earthly high school student stepped through the thermodynamic logic for the existence of hell, debunking key concepts of these ideas.[20]

So, Ramona aimed to start new quantum travel in order to transfer her being outside of the observable universe. After careful deliberation, Ramona decided to distribute several quantum representations of her current lifeform throughout the universe. Her goal? Bring one version of herself to the event horizon of a black hole. Ramona intended to analyze her entry and travel through the black hole into its high-density plasma center and then into the universe that is predicted to be beyond every black hole.[21,22]

Analyzing the events while traveling through a black hole and getting back home presented its own challenges. As time was likely limited for each of her quantum beings' existence, Ramona planned for optimal observational accuracy by using recording devices. These devices would communicate back to Ramona's planet near Messier 13.

Ramona used a time- and distance-independent Boltzmann brain communication tool, which she expected would not be impaired by the black hole's event horizon as long as she could reach the new universe beyond the black hole. In addition, Ramona would be able to travel back to Messier 13 by bringing her handheld portable quantum travel device, which would instantaneously calculate her atomic body composition and transfer it back to her planet.

Again, this would only be feasible if a universe beyond the black hole represented an independent parallel universe where

20 (Keane)
21 (Hamer)
22 (Siegel)

wormhole or quantum-tunnel-like travel between universes was feasible. Ramona considered many of these uncertainties and, despite the risks, decided to start the exploration.

Ramona, thus, transferred her body's atomic composition profile throughout the universe, where she would assemble in compatible environments for shorter or longer time periods. Her physical being on the planet near Messier 13 would remain intact and await her return while coordinating the events and guiding communication.

Soon, she became aware of an activated quantum copy of herself near an infinitely dense black hole in her own galaxy. Messier 13 Ramona referred to her atomic sister that was just assembled with the nickname "RamonaToo."

Following RamonaToo's assembly, the event horizon drew her into the black hole. In the process, she was speeding up and being stretched physically. She could feel her machine being contorted, pulled, twisted and shaken. The experience was remarkable albeit entirely uncomfortable and nauseating. Then, absolute silence. It was as if nothingness had swallowed itself. Shortly thereafter, RamonaToo's communication continued. This made it clear to Messier 13 Ramona that she had entered a new universe beyond the singularity of the black hole.[23]

RamonaToo had traveled at near the speed of light to the center of the black hole where she was being merged with the atomic plasma of vast amounts of matter that had accumulated there over hundreds of millions of years. In the atomic plasma, RamonaToo traveled to what appeared to be the singularity, or infinitely small center point, of the black hole, where she

23 (Hamer)

entered the equivalent of a quantum tunnel. Shuttling through the quantum tunnel, she emerged in open space, illuminated with an intense glow. She was at the core of the plasma.

This core of plasma that enabled a new universe beyond the black hole had been built over time from matter drawn into the black hole. The matter included remnants of atoms that had been part of living creatures on planets, including dinosaur-like lifeforms, lifeforms from levels one through five from all around the galaxy. These remnants now created a coherent and uniform space.

Surprisingly, RamonaToo was able to communicate with this plasma matter, even though her own physical structure had disintegrated. Most striking was the ability to sense awareness of prior lives of these remnants of matter. Organisms that had flourished and withered, planets that had burst in and out of existence, and suns that had become red giants and exploded all shared their past in the space beyond the singularity of the black hole. Remnants of matter were reliving their prior experiences in a shared manner, as all individual atomic structures were lost. Here, a super intellect with memories of past events created a new awareness of the galactic history.

RamonaToo became aware that she could share and communicate with all lifeforms that had existed over hundreds of millions of years. This awareness presented clarity as to the nature of life derived from shared matter. From primordial archaeopteryx[24] to examples of the "dragon thief" dinosaur, all lifeforms had plasma matter representation and a history to share.

24 (Xu 2011)

An infinitely large universe in an infinitely small space. Beyond the black hole, a new universe emerges from its own big bang with new physical limitations on matter's ability to support organic and inorganic lifeforms.

RamonaToo started to communicate with the plasma matter about its insights and experiences. The ability of the plasma to have universal knowledge of the lifeforms comprising its atoms was exhilarating. Better yet, RamonaToo had become part of this. It was as if the plasma held the know-how of all atomic history. Most surprisingly, the plasma could coherently represent the history of atomic lifeforms, whether organic or inorganic.

Struck with awe and appreciation, RamonaToo soon left the plasma center of the wormhole and entered a new universe born from the singularity. An infinitely large universe in an infinitely small space.[25, 26] While lifeforms could assemble in this universe, their atomic structures, their quantum strings, had increased vibrational dimensions. This allowed each new universe to create black holes that represented the origins of yet another universe. It was as if she had encountered the beginning of a big bang by traveling through the singularity.

RamonaToo then found herself transported to a small planet. Inhabitants were few and diverse in physical makeup. Creatures did not pay attention to each other and simply ate and slept while existing in stable communities.

The space-time zone of this universe and planet compared to RamonaToo's prior living was unusual with time being reversed; day by day, everything became younger. What RamonaToo would soon realize was that, having left her universe and now entered this new reality, she was, in essence, looking back at the event horizon from within the black hole.

---

25 (Cantor)
26 (Ferreirós)

Oddly, this had a profound impact on the space-time zone she now lived in.

Just imagine a regular clock that tracks time was transparent and, when looking at it from the front in her original universe, as time passed, the handles moved clockwise or to the right. Looking at this clock from the back, after traveling through the singularity of the black hole and entering a new universe, the same handles of the clock would again travel in a regular circle. However, visualizing the clock from the back, the handles would now turn left or counterclockwise. Thus, time was reversed as defined by the black hole as a future holographic screen.[27]

Going back in time implied that RamonaToo physically became younger and lost her memories and experiences from events that had occurred on prior days. Essentially, this universe and its inhabitants were designed to evaporate and disappear as time passed. So, as the hands moved on the clock, her previous experiences were erased from memory.

During the first day at the new planet, this was not immediately noticeable. However, as time passed, RamonaToo realized that each day was a novel experience without any recollection of what had transpired the day before. Tracking her role on the new planet became impossible as plans disappeared while RamonaToo, day by day, lost memories and experiences. She could only live in the moment but without knowhow of her life on the new planet. RamonaToo felt that she was trapped on a planet where every day led to zero actionable activities.

27 (Bousso and Engelhardt)

Time reversed. When looking at the clock from outside the event horizon (left half of image), the handles on the clock move from right to left as time passes. However, looking at time from within the event horizon, imagining this same clock is being viewed after having passed through the event horizon, we look at the back of it (right half of image). This leads the handles on the clock to move from left to right, moving counterclockwise, reflecting that time is reversed.

As her memories of events in the new universe faded away, she remained aware of the planning completed almost two weeks prior to her quantum travel into the new universe. As a result, RamonaToo decided that she must engage in new quantum travel.

Two options were available to her: quantum travel back to her planet near Messier 13 or travel in this new universe to one of its black holes, where she predicted she would again be led to a new universe. Here, logic implied that time would again reverse and, thus, track forward.

Weighing the options, RamonaToo quickly realized she lacked the equipment to transfer her atomic being throughout this time-reversed universe. Consequently, trying to travel through a black hole in this new universe was simply not feasible. Her only option was to use her portable quantum transporter, define her atomic composition, and return to Messier 13.

This wasn't as simple as just clicking a button on her wrist. The transporter needed to be charged. RamonaToo set out and built a solar energy panel to power the wearable transporter. Every day, when she awoke, her memories were gone, but she came to the same conclusion, made the same plan, and found her transporter being charged. Given low charging efficiency on the planet, the task took almost ninety years as a result, as much earthly time as she had taken since starting planetary explorations.

After ninety years of waiting and living the same day with the same conclusions and the same outcome, her transporter was ready. RamonaToo jabbed her finger at the atomizer button with glee and vigor, left the new universe, and was transported instantly to her planet near Messier 13, where she found her now much older twin sister, the original Ramona. RamonaToo now again stepped through a normal aging process. Her return from the black hole caused her to start a new life, partially reliving the original Ramona's experiences.

The younger Ramona, RamonaToo, was motivated to start her galactic explorations to generate her insights for *I Am Machine: Lesson One – Life without Free Will.* After having returned to her planet near Messier 13, Ramona helped RamonaToo in the activities that had initially guided Ramona's travels to Earth, the black hole, and the new universe. Ramona, thus, guided the younger RamonaToo's travel, as gaining knowledge by reliving prior experiences promised to present an infinite road to discovering the answers to the what, how, and why questions of life.

Chapter 7

FLEETING IDENTITY

The concept of identity for a living organism is often considered inherent to having free will. Reasoning states that you need an identity to be recognized as a unique living organism that can act in its environment, executing on personal choices and, thus, progressing on a path in life.

Ramona considered this carefully. She understood that identity for any living organism needed to be seen in the context of the multitude of other living organisms, each with diverse innate capabilities, living in our universe or in parallel universes beyond our observable existence. Superimposed on this, she added the accepted viewpoint that most organisms are observers of their lives, where decisions originate from an evolutionarily designed and conditioned AGI machine.

Going through these considerations, Ramona was curious as to how others made sense of it all. She had learned while visiting different planets that philosophical ideas, like Earth's metaphysics theory derived from the ancient Greek philosophers, addressed the concept of identity, the nature of consciousness and matter and its relationship to free will. Bringing a range of philosophies together, Ramona concluded that identity, in its simplest definition, is based on the building blocks that create each living organism.

Now that RamonaToo had returned from a parallel universe beyond the singularity of a black hole, she and Ramona discussed their understandings of identity. Sitting across from one another in Ramona's apartment on their home planet, the two women shared their thoughts.

"Well, who is the real Ramona?" Ramona said.

"Or take it further, sister. Is there a single 'real' Ramona? And which criteria do we apply to define that Ramona's identity?"

The two women stared at one another perplexed.

Answering those questions turned out to be challenging, as RamonaToo and Ramona, while deeply aligned on many topics, at times differed in opinion. Both Ramonas soon realized that while they were the same person by design, their experiences and, hence, the training of their unique AGI machines had varied. Ramona had spent decades on Earth. RamonaToo had spent an additional ninety years in a backward time loop in a different universe. As a result, each had developed different preferences.

This was fascinating. Intrigued, Ramona began researching various philosophies on identity. One evening, after a particularly arduous day in the library, Ramona shared what she had learned of the Greek philosophy of Theseus's ship.[28]

"RamonaToo! Sister. The theory of Theseus's ship is quite intriguing. It addresses what it could mean to have an identity. The Greek philosophers Heraclitus and Plato posed the question that, if a ship were built and kept in a harbor, and every

28 (Cohen)

part of the ship was replaced with an identical item, would it be a new ship when done?"

RamonaToo squinted her eyes and stared up into space. Ramona had quickly learned this was her thinking face and knew to give her space as she contemplated.

Several hours later, RamonaToo came to Ramona in the kitchen where she was cooking. "Well…based on personal experiences, replacement of items in real time never recreates the same 'ship' or the same 'person.' Each piece is unto itself new, creating a new whole. So, it would be a new ship. It must be."

Ramona nodded emphatically in agreement.

Their logic was based on the notion that, as time passed while working on the ship, different environmental influences, from light exposure to the people who worked on the ship to the water molecules that kept it afloat, would continuously change and alter its history and experiences. So, it could not be the same ship. It must be a new ship with its own particles and its own history. This now also applied to the Ramonas, who were different personalities.

This logic was striking as the Ramonas had also wondered how the building blocks living beings are made of, from hydrogen and oxygen to carbon and nitrogen or other atoms, are continuously exchanged between living organisms on a given planet over millions of years. To go one step further, each of us is built with carbon and other atoms that were once part of a diverse set of other organisms. From a prehistoric archaeopteryx to undesired characters like Adolf Hitler or fascinating beings like Salvador Dali, our atoms are shared across organisms and across time. In fact, Sam Kean[29], an American author, calculated that, on planet Earth, with every breath one takes, one shares an atom that was once part of Julius Caesar's body.

Similar atoms were also the building blocks of life, though in different historical settings for the Ramonas and other lifeforms on their planet near Messier 13. It was intriguing to consider the ability to track the path taken by these exchangeable atomic building blocks, which, while never being able to create an identical "ship," shared the ability to sustain such diverse lifeforms.

Ramona considered that perhaps the concepts of identity and decision-making were a necessary evolutionary illusion, enabling the various parts of our AGI machines to effectively work in concert in order to prosper in the challenging environments we live in. These philosophical considerations allowed each Ramona to comfortably live independently, sharing a common design while never being confused with being the same person. They viewed themselves as members of a community of creatures that shared and exchanged the same building blocks over hundreds of millions of years.

While free will had been put aside as a philosophical fallacy, the pleasure of being an observing independent machine that executes on a plan and thereby sustains a chain of life events remained a heartwarming experience for the Ramonas.

29 (Kean)

Chapter 8

RAMONA'S CONTINUED EXPLORATION OF THE GALAXY

While RamonaToo engaged in exploring free will on Earth, Ramona and the team made a plan to discover and potentially communicate with inorganic lifeforms in their galaxy. The first exploration involved a detailed review of electrical plasma storms and magnetic fields in the galaxy. They proposed that these storms coordinated information storage and data exchange and that these could represent an inorganic intellect. The bottom line, she considered, is that these storms could be interpreted to perform in the galaxy, between clusters of gas, planets, and other matter, what neurons do in the brain. They modeled that these self-propagating charge distribution and storage changes shared similarities with those occurring in an organic brain, not dissimilar from a neuronal network or a Boltzmann brain.

Ramona and her team considered this a high-risk project, as proving that these charge distributions carried information presented a topic that had been largely ignored by most organic lifeforms. The team had postulated that these electrical plasma storms could represent cognitive powers.

Several examples of electrical plasma storms had been found near the galactic cluster Messier 13. The cluster had a high density of stars with planets where changes in electrical plasma and magnetic field distributions were proposed to store information relating to ongoing planetary events. There were even indications that the electrical plasma storms and magnetic fields effectively exchanged charge distributions throughout the galaxy. Adjacent solar systems near the great globular cluster Messier 13 had also been noted to share electrical plasma storm exchanges. These plasma storms were shown to be associated with selected events in the globular cluster, leading to the unusual model that these might reflect intellect, exhibiting communication skills.

Back on their planet near Messier 13, the team planned to visit one of the most active electrical plasma clusters. As these electrical plasma storms were proposed to carry information exchange capabilities, the team's goal was to determine whether they could influence the behavior of the electrical plasma storms and potentially obtain a response, establishing communication with this putative electrical and magnetic universe, which Ramona hypothesized represented a long-lived Boltzmann intellect. Interestingly, Ramona learned that, even on Earth, evidence was being gathered that electrical stimuli of matter, as proposed for the galaxy, enabled learning, similar to an organic brain's neuronal activity. [30]

To have true impact and to participate in electrical plasma storm mediated communication, the team had been granted access to a spaceship with vast energy production capabilities. This would provide the ship with the capacity to influ-

30 (Purdue University)

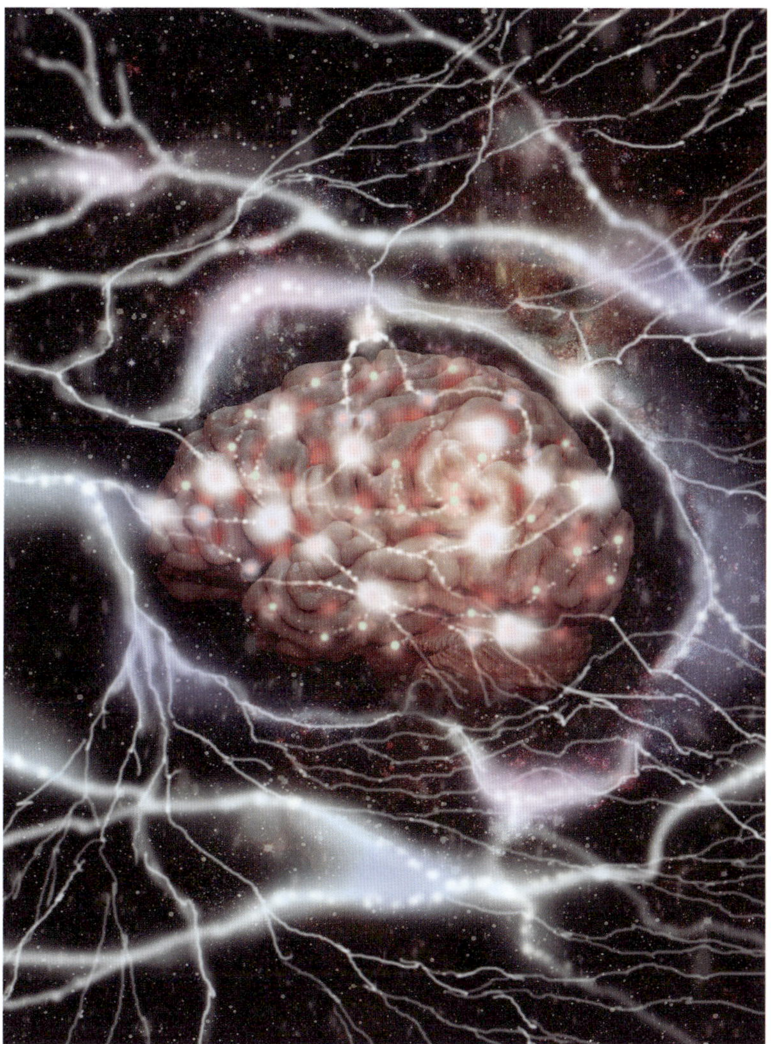

Ramona and the team communicate with the electrical and magnetic plasma centers in the galaxy, receiving critical information from this inorganic intellect.

ence the electrical plasma storms.[31] The spaceship's nuclear fusion capacity allowed the generation of a million zettajoules of energy per second, comparable to ten million times Earth's energy generated per year. This power was needed to impact the electrical plasma storms and allow Ramona's team to explore some form of communication with the galaxy.

Ramona had mapped the distribution of electrical plasma and magnetic gradients, including the location of electrical storm concentration centers in the galaxy, and found that there were oscillating patterns of charge exchanges. These oscillating patterns changed the distribution of stored electrical and magnetic energy. These changes made Ramona aware that the electrical charge distribution in the galaxy seemed to have detailed organization and, apparently, energy transfer rules. It was as if they represented aspects of the functioning of an inorganic lifeform. In their efforts, Ramona and her team located over fifty centers of highly fluctuating electrical plasma and magnetic activity that seemed to influence each other, showing charge distribution dependencies.

Their next observation was that recent charge distribution adjustments correlated with changes in planetary systems that happened as a result of catastrophic impacts due to a meteor hitting a planet and a red giant going dormant. This led to the model that the electrical plasma storms and magnetic energy, including other forms of electrical storms, were documenting planetary events throughout the galaxy. Ramona and her team were learning so much but clearly were only standing at the beginning of an array of new insights and discoveries.

---

31 (Scott)

In addition, electrical plasma storms were seen to influence the atmosphere on planets—for instance, by changing Earth's magnetosphere, triggering displays of the northern lights. This led Ramona to believe that even our galaxy might be considered an inorganic lifeform, an observing creature, tracking and possibly driving numerous changes in galactic organization.

The team decided to perform an experiment by imposing a vast pulse of energy from their spaceship on one of the apparently observing and possibly controlling electrical and magnetic plasma centers. The goal was to measure the response in order to understand current connectivity and then to obtain evidence of galactic electrical and magnetic fields for data storage and await a response that might address the presence of intellect.

Following the injection of one hundred million zettajoules of energy per second over two minutes into one of the over fifty fluctuating energy centers located close to the globular cluster Messier 13, a number of exciting observations were made. After the spaceship initiated the energy pulse, a galactic pulse of energy exchange resulted throughout all the energy centers. The energy oscillations lasted about two minutes, after which a plasma energy pulse was directed at Ramona's spaceship. Ultimately, Ramona and her colleagues became part of an apparent galactic electric information exchange event.

Ramona and her team stood transfixed in their spaceship. Never before had such an experiment been attempted, let alone had such a response been received in return. With a soft, delicate but resounding voice, a galactic intellect spoke to Ramona through Boltzmann-enabled communication.

"We have received your energy message. We understand your attempt to communicate with us, the galaxy. Return to your home planet. When there, begin preparations for weekly communications with us, this galactic intellect. Once back home, your dog, Pinky, will serve as the Boltzmann intermediary of our communication. Pinky has been in touch with us for decades and now will enable our virtual presence."

Ramona turned and stared at her team, her eyes wide with surprise and glowing with hope. On her arrival back home, Ramona was excited to find that her dog, Pinky, would be serving as the Boltzmann brain intermediate controlled by the galaxy. Pinky was a medium-sized dog with incredibly knowing eyes. Ramona's friends had always said that when Pinky was looking at them, it was as if he were reading their minds.

Pinky's role was to ensure that the transfer of information occurred in a socially appropriate manner. This was a behavior at which Pinky was an expert. He was an accommodating, quiet, and observant creature who had, without Ramona's knowledge, been engaged in galactic philosophical communications for almost his entire life.

Pinky, as the philosophical observer of the galactic brain, now became empowered to engage in weekly Boltzmann communications to share information between Ramona and the galaxy. In this manner, Ramona would be kept up to date on major galactic changes in globular cluster functioning and stability. She learned the galaxy planned to enable biological life despite a high frequency of changes in solar radiation that had occurred over the previous thousand years. The awareness of an electrical and magnetic plasma intellect, represented by the galaxy, was a major advancement in the team's understanding of and engagement with intellect throughout the universe.

Ramona recognized that information about the existence of galactic intellect was so powerful that she decided to spread awareness across the galaxies. For Ramona, her team, and human life on earth, the realization that galactic intellect capable of guiding and influencing biological life existed was an eye opener. This summary is Ramona's first step in sharing awareness of these facts.

Ramona realized that Pinky could transmit Boltzmann-like cognitive information, but she had been unaware of the role Pinky played in facilitating communication with the galaxy. Pinky's ability to transmit information was, in itself, surprising and now enabled an influx of information exchange. Most of all, Ramona wanted to understand what it meant for the galaxy to have intellect, to be able to communicate, plan, and explore observations.

How could the galaxy perform such functions? Could a single galaxy be seen as a conscious intellect with intermediary interpreters like Pinky? What did this mean for clusters of galaxies and their living organisms? What did this mean over the long run for the future of the intellectual basis of our galaxy and even the ever-expanding universe with all its galaxies?

Thinking through these observations, Ramona considered it most plausible that the electrical plasma in our galaxy and throughout space had a frequency preference through which it could reach some organisms, such as Pinky. Ramona, in turn, was fortunate that she and Pinky could directly communicate and, hence, share information.

Once clarity had settled on the origin of Ramona's access to galactic intellect, a stream of consciousness resulted about the impact of the cognitive galactic capability. Ramona soon learned that the galaxy was not concerned with the actions of its organic microbiome of which Ramona and Pinky were a part. These were background rumbles, like pleasant music or scents one can enjoy in a socially complex environment. Most of all, the galaxy had, since the beginning of its time, been building a vision of the future, including its own development, the status of its stellar systems, black holes, gas deposits, meteors, supernova explosions, and so many events that defined it as a lifeform.

In addition, the galaxy observed and interacted with other galaxies in the universe. While Boltzmann-like communication, like advanced quantum mechanical computing, was time- and distance-independent, the expansion of our universe made space-derived electrical plasma communication between galaxies a rare event. As a result, the galaxies could be seen as nearly independent cognitive powers that were members of a community of intellect that occupied the entire universe. Their shared ability to observe, project, and calculate future events made these systems possible level-three or level-four inorganic intellects in the scheme of living organisms.

These considerations were eye-openers to Ramona and her colleagues and re-invigorated their interest in learning from the galaxy's insights and the knowledge it gained from being a member of the universe.

The galaxy shared that, from its earliest inception, it had changed and matured as its composition with ever-heavier atoms had altered its makeup and its complexity. The galaxy had vastly expanded from the initial near primordial phase to its current state with stars, black holes, and vibrant plasma currents that manage information, much like an organic brain.

Of course, a critical difference to an organic brain was that the galaxy broadly continued to mature its physical makeup and, hence, its intellect throughout its life. This allowed ever more complex information management and interpretations. These, in turn, facilitated calculating and making predictions with regard to the galaxy's and the universe's current and future state. In these efforts, galaxies had the ability to share cognitive powers and present an unimaginable capability to observe and guide the universe. Ramona considered that the evolving galaxy could mature over time to become a level-one or level-two inorganic intellect.

Chapter 9

BEYOND THE EDGES OF OUR UNIVERSE

Ramona remained restless but was excited by the wealth of discoveries she and her team had made. The impact of discovering galactic intellect was profound, and the group celebrated the discoveries with lengthy philosophical discussions. The findings changed their understanding of life and what it meant to have cognitive power. Also, the origin of the cognitive powers had been put in the context of the limitations of the powers of organic life on different planets.

While the discoveries were mesmerizing, Ramona ended up with more headaches and sleepless nights as the findings only moved the considerations for the existence of organic life and our intellect one step further down the line of logical reasoning. They never resolved the basic questions that focus on: Why is there life? Where does it move to over billions of years? And why does the universe exist?

Ramona became ever more determined to tackle these questions with intensity, and she started drafting a practical plan to make next steps in unraveling this daunting array of thoughts, which had kept her occupied since childhood. Both frustration and anxiety were part of these considerations, as every new discovery resulted in more tantalizing questions. While Ramona had gained profound knowledge, it did not appear that there was light at the end of the tunnel of reasoning.

Ramona and the team contemplated the discoveries and the unknowns and ended up with varying opinions on the importance of the remaining questions. Some team members found great satisfaction in knowing their position, capabilities, and limitations, which, by all means, were enormously enabling. The findings were being published in diverse language releases of *I Am Machine: Lesson One* on different planets. The resulting societal and political impact was profound, helping stabilize societies by enabling guided conditioning of populations of organic lifeforms. The self-centered importance many organisms had enjoyed was pleasantly eroded, and key topics relating to societal well-being and care for the empathic and smart conditioning of populations became part of every world that embraced the findings.

While these advances were extensive, the core questions relating to the why, what, and how we do what we do remained unanswered. Following months of implementation of data sharing and building educational programs for lifeforms in the galaxy, the galactic team split into two groups. One group focused on translation and dissemination of the information to all cognitively enabled level-three and level-four organisms. This task was vast, given the billions of planetary lifeforms in the galaxy. While this team refined its methods for sharing information, Ramona and Pinky decided to separate from the group to explore the basic questions addressing the reasons for existence, an ever more daunting task.

Ramona decided that clarity on her role as a living being could be settled if she could travel beyond the edges of our universe and, from there, observe the why, what, and how of life. She anticipated that exploring space outside our universe could present unexpected insights.

As classical travel could not accomplish this, Ramona rebuilt the device that calculated her current atomic makeup in preparation for travel in the universe. She also included the handheld transporter, which would allow her to return to her planet near Messier 13 whenever needed. Finally, rather than send this information with advanced quantum computing to a specific planet, Ramona planned to disseminate the information randomly throughout the universe.

At some locations, like in empty space, Ramona's body would be expected to survive only minutes, while at other locations, she could live for years. Ramona, thus, decided to distribute her atomic composition as a quantum lifeform. Her original physical being would again remain functional on her planet near Messier 13. The distributed Ramonas that became organic lifeforms then could either transport back to Messier 13 or, pending the circumstance, share Boltzmann-like cognitive intelligence with Ramona and Pinky on Messier 13. So, Ramona's travels throughout and beyond the universe continued.

The first release of Ramona's being throughout the universe led to a remarkable set of observations based on the assembly of Ramona at two separate locations. These events provided great clarity on the nature of our universe.

After her first assembly, Ramona found herself in our universe near what appeared to be the very edges of space.

There, Ramona could see a horizon of galaxies on one side and the absolute absence of any matter, galaxies, or other matter in the opposite direction. Ramona figured that she had indeed traveled to the edge of the universe and, from there, could view the absolute nothingness beyond.

However, in this vast "nothing," over the horizon, in the uncanny distance, was a mere spot of light that appeared to indicate the presence of matter at an unmeasurable distance from our universe. Ramona was transfixed and mesmerized by the possibility that outside our well-organized flat universe, there could be other sources of matter or energy beyond our point of observation. Following those insights, Ramona's body disintegrated.

Ramona's second encounter was by far the most illuminating. Ramona again found herself facing our universe from a distance, seeing matter in her field of vision and absolute nothingness on the other side. Again, this indicated that our universe expanded into existing empty space.

In this status, Ramona realized that her body was continually changing, as if matter anti-matter particles, as can be detected at the event horizon of a black hole, were reassembling her physique. For example, one of her legs would disappear only to rebuild seconds later. These events happened spontaneously without warning and caused no discomfort. Ramona watched this occur as anyone on Earth, or her planet, would watch a fish swimming in an aquarium—with curiosity and interest.

Then, it appeared that the expansion of the flat universe was speeding up. Although Ramona appeared stationary, the density of galaxies in the flat universe diminished rapidly as they were moving apart at near the speed of light while expanding towards Ramona. As this phenomenon was ongoing, a bright spot of light in the area of empty space became clearer and started showing details of galactic structures. Ramona realized that the universe she had lived in was expanding fast, possibly because Ramona's space-time zone had altered, and hundreds of millions of years seemed to happen in seconds for Ramona.

The spot of light in the empty space came closer and closer to Ramona, making it appear that this was a separate universe with enormous galactic density. This immediately indicated to Ramona that parallel universes, in addition to the black hole-enabled universe, were a reality. Given the speed over which these events were observed, Ramona realized that her position in the apparently empty space had unveiled a unique space-time zone from where events that take hundreds of millions of years could be viewed in seconds.

These two events had a profound impact on Ramona's understanding of our universe. She was now familiar with organic and inorganic lifeforms having comparable roles in our universe. What stood out was that the need to observe and respond was not unique to organic life. In fact, all matter in the universe seemed to contribute and be part of life and its intellectual presentation. Next, Ramona acknowledged that the wealth of living creatures in our universe requires that we rationalize our roles in this system. As conditioned machines that often live for millennia in isolation on a planet without interacting with other living systems, our operational freedom and intellect remain limited.

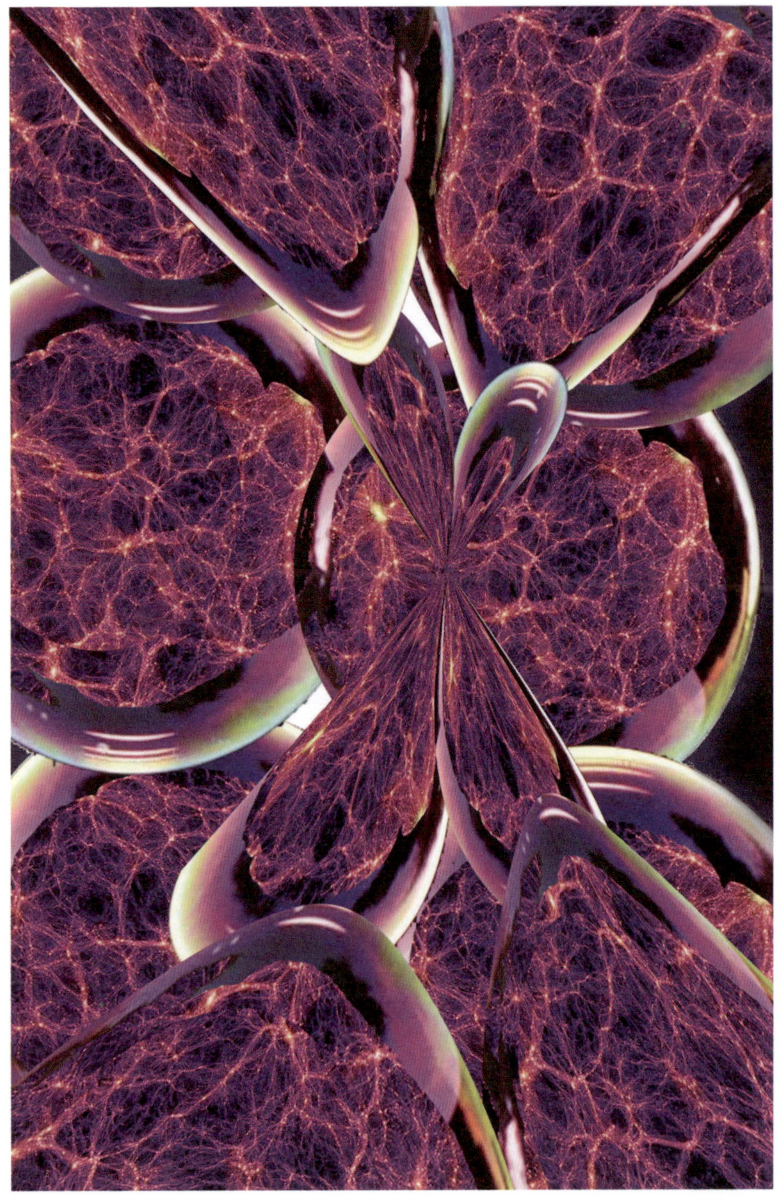

Ramona discovers parallel universes and expands her understanding of life in the vast complexity of space unveiled.

Finally, the outlets into a parallel universe, or integral to our universe when considering Ramona's black hole experience, outline that we have only just scratched the surface of our being. As the Dalai Lama stated, it is "the universe in a single atom." This mental concept will help level-three and level-four organic lifeforms to build societies that admire all forms of life while acknowledging the importance of the temporary existence of each organic life-enabled observer.

PART 3

ENABLING MATHEMATICAL PRINCIPLES

Chapter 10

LIFE – A ONE-WAY VOYAGE FOR ANY INDIVIDUAL

Ramona found herself again standing in front of a podium but now at an intergalactic council. The beings in front of her represented machines of all different types, shapes, sizes, and smells. Her heart felt full knowing that she had coordinated bringing these beings together.

Ramona was now many, many years older. Her hair was a bright silver and gray. Her skin, no longer tight, oily, and scaly, fell softly on her bones. She remained strong of heart and was a vibrant force of nature on her planet and in her community. She had become a well-respected, though not always loved, scientific and philosophical expert across galaxies. Ramona took a sip of water, cleared her throat, and began what she knew to be one of her last symposiums. Below is a copy of her speech notes.

Reincarnation and eternal life, as aspired by many organic lifeforms, are inherent to numerous philosophies and religions. Some of these philosophies shed light on life's long-term mission. This, of course, assumes that there is a fundamental mission to the existence of the universe, human life, and other lifeforms. Let me clarify how some aspects can be debunked:

1. The interesting concept of identity (see Chapter 7) and the ability to return with the same identity to relive a life in our universe can mathematically be shown not to be feasible. For instance, the notion that, given infinite time, we can rebuild all past structures of atoms that performed selected actions appears attractive at first. However, varying types of infinities exist, and amazingly, even Earth's scientists have proven that some infinities are larger than others.[32,33] *These transfinite number series explain that current events and complexities created over time always surpass the complexity of recapitulating events that aim to rebuild every molecular detail. Therefore, the complexities created by lifeforms over time, combined with quantum uncertainty, seem to prevent an exact repeat or reincarnation of past events, even if infinite time is applied. Hence, mathematically reliving exact events does not seem viable, even given infinite time in any galaxy or universe.*

2. The consequence of this logic is that life and its actions represent one-time events driven by quantum mechanical uncertainties, whether we consider parallel universes or not.

3. The notion that a rerun of a life lived is not feasible is helpful as it erodes the assumption of a recurring identity for a lifeform.

32 (Cantor)
33 (Ferreirós)

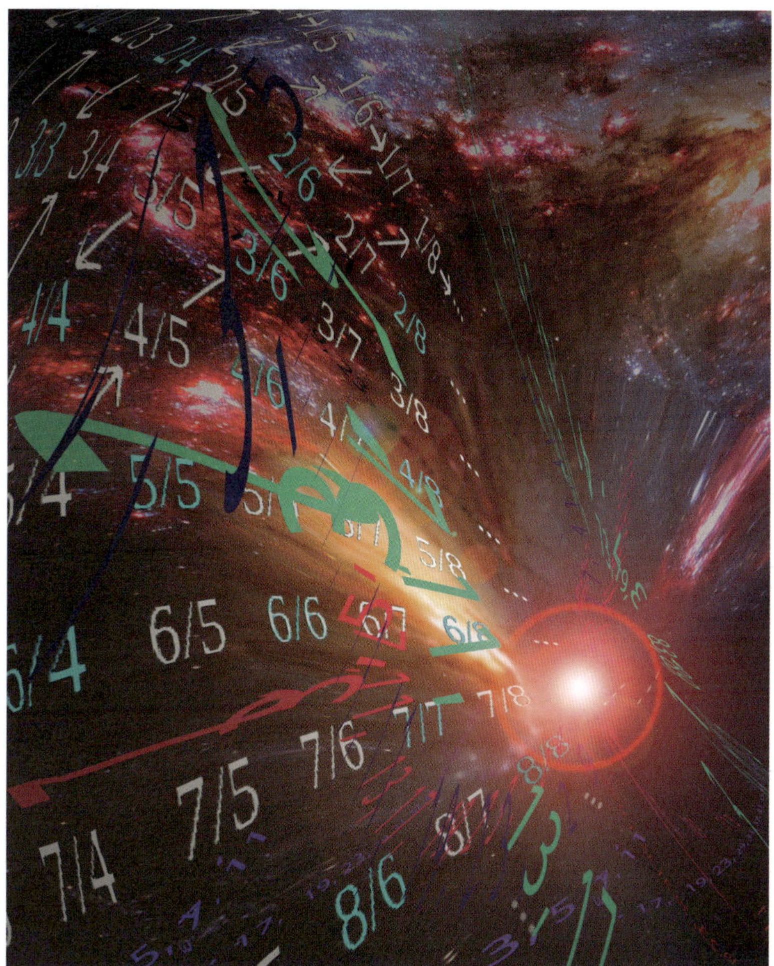

Infinite time. Cantor's infinities help explain life's opportunities and limitations. Infinities exist in different sizes, and some infinitely large number series are always bigger than others. This discovery has exciting philosophical implications, impacting diverse concepts active in human theories of life or the ability to recreate life after death of an organic being.

4. Of course, our lives represented by a simulated digital universe could offset this logic, as such a digital world could dictate life's actions and be rebuilt. Another version of this is our world as a holographic simulation screen, which, again, could be digitally built. Finally, the Boltzmann brain hypothesis, from Earth's year 1872, presents an opportunity for continuity of consciousness or reliving life's experiences. This hypothesis could be brought a step further by postulating that a Boltzmann brain could spontaneously arise

Mathematics and infinities. Some infinities are bigger than others, where the Boltzmann brain hypothesis may present an opening to continued transient cognitive abilities.

that carries an individual's thoughts but also captures the thoughts of his/her partners, thereby opening doors to all thoughts ever conceived and making them transparent to that couple. More compellingly, one can conceive that such spontaneous intellect that entails the consciousness of innumerable people or different lifeforms could exist for a fraction of time. I would consider this shared intellect, a pleasant phantom of intelligence. Given the Boltzmann brain option, we have a theoretical solution to shared cognition and awareness. For example, my first Boltzmann encounter eliminated time and distance, allowing two minds to instantly share awareness of a single event. It was beautiful, unnerving, and fascinating!

5. Even more notably, the interactions arising from other information managing systems, like "smart electrical storms" that carry digital information in our universe, may similarly give rise to intellect shaped by physical matter with the power of a Boltzmann-like brain.

These ideas and the Boltzmann brain hypothesis may be interesting given the following considerations:

i) When one dies, time stops for the deceased.

ii) For the deceased, the next awareness, given infinite time, is that the deceased intellect may spontaneously and transiently re-exist, fully aware of its past activities, whether as a Boltzmann brain or a "smart electrical storm," creating collective wisdom through universal shared intellect.

iii) Boltzmann intellect can exist that gathers the thoughts of many living creatures. As stated earlier, consider that in this Boltzmann-like brain, every thought, once experienced, is visible to everyone, every human or other lifeform. This would allow collective intellect to become a reality. Hence, when considering reincarnation, one could argue that Boltzmann presents a solution to even silly ideas, such as recurring cognitive existence.

While I have explained the notion that most living organisms manage life without free will, operating as conditioned AGI machines, it is important to clarify that this model does not imply determinism, as in completely predefining all future actions of the machine. It simply states that lifeforms are defined by the machine each represents and that they are the observers of the machine's actions, thus enabling its functionality. Hence, this proposed state of the machine does not necessarily include a deterministic path through life, and even though philosophies of super determinism exist, we await proof. Clarity of these concepts will help guide living organisms throughout their lifespan.[34,35]

I concluded that matter can build observers in our universe. The observer's actions are one-time events aimed at maintenance and propagation of each lifeform. As the universe itself is a lifeform, we need to accept our observer role in this vast cognitive space.

I next considered the fate of our universe. Where are we heading? To address this question, I calculated, based on the

34 (Hossenfelder and Palmer)
35 (Horgan)

atomic density of our universe, how many atomic movements have occurred over every microsecond since the beginning of time in the space we know as our universe. These considerations are, of course, essential to the creation of life as we understand it.

I used a standard measure defined by the size of an atom (estimated at 10^{-10} meters). The goal is to define how, over time, atomic matter has aggregated to create cognitive powers and forecast the future of our universe. The bottom line is that we have a narrow window of opportunity in time to enjoy cognition as we know it.

Consider that our universe has 10^{80} atoms and, to date, our universe is 1.35×10^{39} atom-sized space units long. In this universe, since the beginning of time, the atoms have had the opportunity for 4.5×10^{101} atomic microsecond movement/reaction events. The total number of atomic space units in our universe, assuming it is a sphere, measures 2.8×10^{117}. These numbers are astounding, but they are just numbers that allow us to conceptualize space and its evolution.

It's simplest to realize that we can capture this complexity of atomic movements in our universe numerically over every microsecond since its existence. These values, to enable life, likely have an optimum over time, where atomic density and microsecond movement/reaction events dictate how matter interacts to create higher order structures. We can assume that creating galaxies and higher order structures required a specific density of atoms in space. As we cannot assume a uniform distribution of matter throughout the universe, and since the universe is expanding at an accelerating pace, we can predict that the current distribution of matter defines the future of most atomic interactions. In these considerations, the spontaneous occurrence of matter anti-matter particles is not taken into account.

To keep this simple, I assume that our current point of observation at 2.8 x 10^{117} atomic space units is our "sweet spot" for organic life given 10^{80} atoms. So, what will the universe look like once we are at 4.18 x 10^{117} atomic space units, which will be well over fourteen billion years from now?

Based on current knowhow, I predict that a bell-shaped curve, tracing atomic microsecond events versus atomic space units over time, describes the ability of matter to create higher order cognitive structures. Hence, eventually, dilution of matter in the ever-expanding universe is predicted to prevent productive molecular interactions and, thus, become too cold to sustain life. Only the escape through black holes may create access to alternative realities, each with their own metrics. I predict that once we reach 4.18 x 10^{117} atomic space units, we will have spent many billions of years since today's events, our stars will have died, and we will have ended life as we know it.

RAMONA'S CLOSING REMARKS

For countless years, equivalent to many earthly lifetimes, I questioned whether free will was a genuine human lifeform capability or a self-indulgent fantasy. By analyzing the design limitations of human lifeforms and comparing these to other organisms in our universe, I have helped define the free will limitations. A simple conclusion is that the AGI machine responds to the impulses it receives as defined by its design, genetic makeup, and conditioning. Its preferences, decisions, and resulting actions are a result of complex mathematics enabled by AI but not of limitless response choices. An extreme interpretation of this model is that we are the observers of the actions taken by our AGI machines. In the end, I have concluded that the free will concept is a fallacy, where pseudo–free will can be considered an educationally enabling preservation of a rescue concept to promote a sense of self beyond the truth.

Now that I have accomplished part of my initial goal, a second objective is to help humans and other lifeforms accept the notion that they are members of a universe of living creatures where planet Earth and even our galaxy are living organisms with cognitive powers. Finally, members of this repertoire of life, including humans, can be considered part of their planet's—for instance, Earth's—microbiome. I anticipate that accepting these concepts will be enabling to any lifeform's cognitive maturation.

I look forward to the next educational visit of our galactic exploration team in support of an ever-maturing planet Earth.

Science and Fiction for Earthly and Extraterrestrial Intellect

ACKNOWLEDGMENTS

Ramona is grateful for feedback received in preparing the release of *I Am Machine: Lesson One*. Specifically, she wants to acknowledge the contributions from Sasja Tse, Sea-Jay Van der Ploeg, Chen Bernards, Halley Young, and Edward Costello, who provided insightful comments. In addition, Lauren Green, Theodor Vogels, Michael Weiden, Caroline Van der Ploeg, Mary Lee, Ru-Yao Van der Ploeg, Andre Bernards, Marcy MacDonald, Peter Jarvis, Charles Cantor, Bud Mishra, Misha Shchepinov, Doris Tse, Shubh Sharma, Sheila DeWitt, Shashi Shashidhar, Andrea Olsen, Tony Czarnik, Larry Gold, Lex Van der Ploeg, and Raymond Van Aalst, as well as the earthly canines Sir Inspector Carbo, George Clooney, and Ramona's canine Pinky and, of course, Nimble Bee were enormously helpful in providing manuscript and illustration/design input.

REFERENCES

Ludwig Boltzmann. Brain hypothesis (1872); https://en.wikipedia.org/wiki/Boltzmann_brain#Spontaneous_formation

Raphael Bousso and Netta Engelhardt. New Area Law in General Relativity. Phys. Rev. Lett. 115, 081301 – Published 18 August 2015

George Cantor. Transfinite series [1915) https://en.wikipedia.org/wiki/Transfinite_number

Marc S. *Cohen, (2004). "Identity, Persistence, and the Ship of Theseus". faculty.washington.edu. Retrieved 2019-03-15*

Leroy Cronin and Sara Imari Walker. Beyond Prebiotic Chemistry. Science, 2016; 352; 1174-1175

J. Ferreiros. "What Fermented in Me for Years": Cantor's Discovery of Transfinite Numbers. Historica Mathematica 22 (1995), 33-42

R. Feynman, R. Leighton, M. Sands. Lectures on Physics. Addison-Wesley Publishing Company (1964) Volumes, 1, 2, 3.

Ben Goertzel, Artificial General Intelligence: Concept, State of the Art, and Future Prospects. Journal of Artificial General Intelligence 5(1) 1-46, 2014

Green and Lavesson, Developmental medicine & child neurology. Volume 61, Issue 10 October 2019. Pages 1120

Ernst Haeckel. The Monist: Vol. 3, No. 2 (January 1893), pp. 234-257 (24 pages)

Ashely Hamer. There might be a Universe inside every black hole. https://www.discovery.com/science/Universe-Inside-Every-Black-Hole August 2019

Sam Harris, 2012, Free Will: https://www.samharris.org/blog/the-illusion-of-free-will

Sabine Hossenfelder and Tim Palmer. Rethinking Superdeterminism. Front. Phys., 06 May 2020. https://doi.org/10.3389/fphy.2020.00139

John Horgan. Does Quantum Mechanics Rule our free Will? Scientific American, 2022. https://www.scientificamerican.com/article/does-quantum-mechanics-rule-out-free-will/

D.A. Hume. Treatise of Human Nature. Oxford; New York, NY: Oxford University Press (2000).
Google Scholar

Sam Kean Caesar's Last Breath Published: 12/07/2018 ISBN: 97817841 62931

Margie Keane. Hell. explained by a chemistry student 2021 https://www.chapala.com/elojo/2016-issues/182-articles-2015/april-2015/2925-hell-explained-by-a-chemistry-student

R. Kuraoka. 10 Scientifically Possible Extraterrestrial Lifeforms (2019) https://listverse.com/2019/02/19/10-scientifically-possible-extraterrestrial-life-forms/

Andrei Linde. Sinks in the Landscape, Boltzmann Brains, and the Cosmological Constant Problem, Journal of Cosmology and Astroparticle Physics, 0701 (2007) 022

B. Libet, C.A. Gleason, E.W. Wright, D.K. Pearl. Time of conscious intention to act in relation to onset of cerebral activity (readiness-potential). The unconscious initiation of a freely voluntary act. Brain 1983 Sep;106 (Pt 3):623-42.

Emily M. Livingston, Linda S. Siegel & Urs Ribary. Developmental dyslexia: emotional impact and consequences. Australian Journal of Learning Difficulties. 21 Jun 2018. ISSN: 1940-4158 (Print) 1940-4166 (Online) Journal homepage: https://www.tandfonline.com/loi/rald20

J. E. Lovelock (1972). "Gaia as seen through the atmosphere". Atmospheric Environment. 6 (8): 579–580. Bibcode:1972 AtmEn...6..579L. doi:10.1016/0004-6981(72)90076-

Caterina Mosti and Emil F. Coccaro. Mild traumatic brain injury and aggression, impulsivity and history of other and self-directed aggression. J Neuropsychiatry Clin Neurosci. 2018; 30(3): 220–227. doi:10.1176/appi.neuropsych.17070141

Other 1: https://www.hpe.com/us/en/what-is/artificial-intelligence.html

Purdue University 2022: https://www.labmanager.com/news/using-electricity-to-find-materials-that-can-learn-29245

Robert Sapolsky. Behave: The Biology of Humans at our Best and Worst. Penguin Press (2017)

D.E. Scott. (2006) The electric Sky. Plasma and electricity in space. ISBM 0-9772851-1-1.

E. Siegel. Did a Black Hole give rise to our Universe? https://www.forbes.com/sites/startswithabang/2020/11/03/did-a-black-hole-give-birth-to-our-universe/ (2020)

Tommy Tomlinson. The Weight I carry. https://www.theatlantic.com/health/archive/2019/01/weight-loss-essay-tomlinson/579832/ (2019)

Lex Van der Ploeg and Raymond Van Aalst. God's Retirement: Lesson Zero. An Illustrated Comic for Believers and Infidels" (Amazon) (2014).

W. Williams, P. Chitsabesan, S. Fazel, T. McMillan, N. Hughes, M. Parsonage, J. Tonks. Traumatic brain injury: a potential cause of violent crime? Lancet Psychiatry. 2018 October; 5(10): 836–844. doi:10.1016/S2215-0366(18)30062-2.

Xing Xu et al., 2011, Nature. 475 (7357): 465–470.

Konrad Zuse. Rechnender Raum, Friedrich Vieweg & Sohn, Braunschweig, 1969.

ABOUT THE AUTHORS

Lex Van der Ploeg's religious upbringing led him to search for answers to the meaning of life, which inspired the publication of *I Am Machine*. Lex is actively involved in writing a series of novels on the philosophy of life from a scientific, physics, and mathematical perspective. Having worked as a tenured faculty member at Columbia University as well as in the pharmaceutical and biotechnology industry, Lex's expertise has included the development of diagnostics and therapeutics for cancer, neurodegenerative disorders, metabolic disorders, and infectious diseases.

Raymond van Aalst graduated cum laude from several art academies in the Netherlands and started an illustration company in 1980. He creates, sells, and publishes oil paintings, lithographs, etchings, cartoons, and drawings worldwide. As a gifted dreamer, Raymond is able to quickly conjure up and process complex images. His curiosity and broad interests have made him a visual intellectual with philosophical depth, where thinking through illustrations enabled by words helps clarify insights for himself and for others.

Lex Van der Ploeg and Raymond van Aalst have also published the satirical illustrated comic titled *God's Retirement: Lesson Zero*. This book, which further explores life and religion, is available for purchase on Amazon.

Acceptance of the free will fallacy philosophy is supported by an earlier publication, *God's Retirement: Lesson Zero – An Illustrated Comic for Believers and Infidels,* which explains the carbon-based view for the origin of life. Coming to grips with the notion that we are atom-based living organisms is enabled by Richard Feynman who stated in 1963, "There is nothing that living things can do that cannot be understood from the point of view that they are made of atoms acting according to the laws of physics." Also, numerous publications on free will discuss its misconceptions (*e.g.*, Harris 2012). Ramona and her friends, similarly, discovered a path where faith in manmade gods is replaced with an agnostic philosophy, where life is viewed in a science and futuristic fantasy enabled manner.

The graduates of Lesson One from the College of Alien Faculty can now expect Lesson Two online in the not-too-distant future.